Don't Forget Me

by Bella Van Winkle

Blue Forge Press

Port Orchard ✿ Washington

Don't Forget Me
Copyright 2019
by Bella Van Winkle

First eBook Edition January 2020
First Print Edition January 2020
Second Print Edition January 2023

ISBN 978-1-59092-923-0

Cover design by Brianne DiMarco

For information about film, reprint or other subsidiary rights, contact blueforgegroup@gmail.com

Blue Forge Press is the print division of the volunteer-run, federal 501 (c)3 nonprofit company, Blue Forge Group, founded in 1989 and dedicated to bringing light to the shadows and voice to the silence. We strive to empower storytellers across all walks of life with our four divisions: Blue Forge Press, Blue Forge Films, Blue Forge Gaming, and Blue Forge Records. Find out more at www. BlueForgeGroup.com

Blue Forge Press
7419 Ebbert Drive Southeast
Port Orchard, Washington 98367
blueforgepress@gmail.com
360-550-2071 ph.txt

to Him
who gave me a chance
to dream

acknowledgements

This book would not have been real without the help of my editor, Brianne, and my publisher, Blue Forge Press. Thank you for helping me make my book baby real.

I want to thank my sister Ruby, who was able to talk me down from my unreasonable thoughts. You never stopped believing in me. Thank you for loving me.

Thank you Julie El Fattal, who listened and read this book when it was just beginning. You let me ramble and cry over these pages. You are the best friend I could ever ask for.

Thanks Mom and Dad, who came with me to all the tough stuff and pushed me to be the best I could be. Thank you family, who supported and boasted me despite everything.

Thank you friends, including but not limited to Mia Tukey, Jamie Stout, Meghan Ngo, Emily Comstock and everyone who helped quell my busy thoughts.

Thank you God, who not only yanked me from the brink, but also handed every opportunity to my oblivious face.

Finally, thank *you*, Reader. This book has been written in stolen moments, but it was not the book that saved me—it was me who saved myself. I hope you find hope from Eryn and Parker.

Dreams stay on your pillow until you *live*.

content warning

This book includes fictional depictions or mentions of: suicide, self-harm, child abuse, and domestic abuse. Those who are sensitive to these themes or struggling with any of these issues may want to read and discuss it with a trusted friend or adult, or may find that this book is not right for them.

introduction

I've always dreamt of writing a book young. A bunch of words that created a story, attached to my name.

I went through most of my life avoiding mirrors, praying to God that he would change who I was, make me look better. He didn't, and I didn't understand why.

I made it to freshman year, and I ended up at a school I didn't want to be at. I was a freshman, a ninth grader, so of course, I was terrified. There were all these people with scowls on their faces, headphones plugged into their ears to block everything out. I was the same age as the sophomores, but I was a grade below. That meant that if something went wrong and I was the only freshman there, I would have been blamed.

I was in a special help class for math (which meant I had two periods of math instead of one) and a science class I hated, but worst of all was Spanish class.

I have an overactive amygdala, which means that social anxiety runs rampant in my head.

Spanish meant learning a new language, and that meant that I had to speak in front of the class. How I felt about that had no place in the classroom.

Every day, I woke up and went to school, walked through the hallways with a scowl permanently planted on my face and earbuds plugged into my ears, and I eventually stopped feeling angry. I stopped feeling sad or lonely, I stopped feeling in general. When I did feel anything, I felt anger. It was better than feeling numb, so I took it.

I got to the point where on the bus ride to school, I prayed to my God, asking him to make a car hit my side of the bus and save my sister, who was on the other side of the aisle. He never did and I hated him for it.

I've written a book before, but it was a copy of one of my favorite books at the time, a pure plagiarism with different characters. It is gone from existence.

I had no stable friends or a stable mentality, but I had good grades, and that meant that my teachers never bothered to notice. I stopped talking about me, and I fully believed I was useless.

I remember the moment I started writing *Don't Forget Me*. I've always been a storyteller. There are dozens of almost finished stories in notebooks and books in my shelves to show for it. I had taken a regular composition notebook out of my family's school supply cupboard. It was the first thing I wrote in there, the beginning pages to *Don't Forget Me*.

I wrote the most during Spanish class, only stopping to talk in front of the class and panic for hours afterwards. It was a way to escape, and these people wrote themselves. I was brought along with them, and when my pencil hit the paper, I no longer had to think. I didn't have to remember where I was, or what I felt like- all that mattered to me was how they felt.

I carried that notebook around, writing poems in the pages in between, and when I got through the full notebook, the covers were soft and falling apart. I started a new one, and then another, and another, and another.

I didn't realize this at the time, but at first, I wrote this about two boys because I wanted to prove that not all Christians were against this type of love. I then wrote because I needed a happy ending, I needed to prove to myself that I would be alright.

And then, I was writing for you, dear reader. I wanted you to see this and believe that you would be okay. I could picture you in my head, I imagined what it would be like talking in front of a group of you, and I knew exactly what I would say.

I went to therapy after I started writing, I got better, I

was able to look myself in the eyes and smile. I knew that God had wanted me to write this, despite those who disagreed. I have learned how to structure my own belief in Him, and because of Him, I am alive and well.

I have dealt with suicidal thoughts and the aftermath of a suicide. I didn't know them, but I cried for them all the same. I saw the reaction they had, the whole school, and I knew what I had to do.

I wrote this for you. So you will have something to believe in. It will not be easy, the path to life (it never is), but it is worth it.

Believe me. It will be worth it.

Don't Forget Me

by Bella Van Winkle

"Silence is where we truly fall in love."

—Bridgett Devoue

chapter one

I haven't killed anyone, I swear

Eryn

My phone buzzed loudly on my bedside table, jolting me out of a restless sleep.

I stared at the ceiling for a moment, trying to find the energy to turn over and respond to whatever Cherry had sent me now.

How did I know it was Cherry? Because she's the only one crazy enough to wake up at six in the morning. If I knew anything about my best friend, I knew that she was insane in every possible meaning.

I had been dreaming something... what was it? Something important, I could feel it. I should've been able to remember, but dreams were tricky things, slipping and sliding out of my grasp like fish underwater.

It was easier to give up than try to remember.

I turned over, grabbing my phone with heavy hands, still blinking bleary sleep from my heavy eyes. I signed in, groaning at the immensely bright screen.

Oh, yeah, this was a great reason to wake me up at six on a Friday. Sure, I had to wake up anyway, but that doesn't mean I wanted to wake up to this.

I swiped away Cherry's hints for finding a boyfriend, groaning when I accidentally clicked on the link she had sent and followed it to a dating site for gay men.

She never gives up does she?

She's just like how my mom used to be. My mom used to be very obvious when she was hinting towards something she wanted me to do, or something she thought would be cool for me to do for her, and Cherry was exactly like that. Mom doesn't really act that way anymore. She's very subdued now, which wasn't bad I guess, but it's also not great.

My mom would support me through anything, even the whole 'being gay' thing—she'd love me even if I killed someone. Which I haven't.

Cherry, however, was more excited than anyone. She'd always been obsessed with finding me love, so this was just another challenge for her, a way to force her 'love-loving soul' into action.

There was no point in telling my dad even if he was here. He skipped town when I was in middle school, and I have no idea where he would be. I didn't really care enough to tell him anyway. It'd been so long since I last saw him that I didn't really remember what he looked like, but again, I didn't care enough to find out.

Nothing in the world would make me tell my stepdad, or as I like to call him, Stepmonster.

Don't get me started on him. He married my mom, and a month into their disgustingly poisonous relationship, he became the worst guy on the planet. I don't know if it was possible to know a more monstrous guy. He's good at manipulating her though, so for now, we stay terrorized by him. There was a certain tone in his voice, something that makes Mom afraid to even try to get away from him. I hear it too sometimes, but he mostly makes me mad. Nothing he could ever do would scare me like he used to.

I rubbed my eyes as I got out of bed, sniffing clothes on the floor until I found something decent enough to wear to face this horrid day.

I peeked through the blinds, wincing at the gentle misting rain, knowing that Cherry would be complaining about this for the entire day. But even so, the way the little bit of sunlight that shone through the thick clouds caught the raindrops as they fell was a sight I would never get tired of.

I rolled my eyes when Stepmonster's voice rolled through the cracks in my door from the living room. He's hungover. He always was, there's nothing new about that.

My foot hits a brown bag as I open my door. I smiled sadly at the lunch bag Mom packed for me and grabbed it, making my way out of the house as quickly as possible. Shaking it, I could tell that she had packed me a sandwich and dropped a few dollars in so that I would be able to buy something else. She didn't exactly have the time to make me a full lunch, after all.

Mom wanted me out of the house as soon as I woke up, which is a normal occurrence now, but it's just the way she said goodbye that hurt every time. It tore me up to see her wave through the living room windows every day instead of hugging me goodbye, but I learned a long time ago not to mess with her.

Every mom has a superpower, and hers were her eyes. She could look at you and see exactly what you were going to do, and she was able to make you feel so guilty about doing it that you'd just forgo it completely. It definitely was a superpower, one that I had been subjected to often over the years.

As I pulled my car onto the road, I checked my reflection quickly.

My brown hair was messy which isn't new. The bags under my eyes have almost disappeared, strangely. I guess the forced facemasks from Cherry have worked.

My skin's always been relatively clear, a blessing I didn't take for granted, so it didn't look like anything was amiss at the moment. My dark brown eyes seemed a bit lighter today, something Cherry will also mention.

I sighed and flipped the mirror closed, turning on the music and cranking it up.

Back to senior year. Back to high school, the best place in the world, says nobody.

My car wheels rumbled underneath me as I turned the wheel, doing my best to drown out every insolent thought that threatened to take over, but just like always, I failed.

That disgusting man. If I could, I'd beat him to a pulp, and I'd send him to jail while laughing, but my mom was always home, and so was he. There's no way I could get him out without him trying to manipulate her, or blame my actions on her. I guess for now, everything stays the same, as much as I hated it.

Cherry walked up to me, her usual smirk replaced by a slightly guilty expression.

I rolled my eyes. I could already smell her upcoming guilty favor.

The school hallway was nearly empty, but still, Cherry finds a way to bump into someone before making her way to me. The hallway filled with the scent of apples as Cherry's perfume grew stronger the closer she came to me.

"Hey Eryn!" she started, flashing finger guns at me. "My best friend in the whole world, the one who holds the key to my heart—"

"What do you want?" I demanded, closing my locker door to watch her.

"What makes you think I need anything?" she asked, adjusting her belt guiltily.

I waved my hand in front of my nose. "It smells like desperation."

She laughed, leaning against the long wall of lockers. "Maybe you're just being all moody, like normal."

"I am not moody," I exclaimed, crossing my arms. Someone next to me began to walk quicker as I scowled at

Cherry, and she shot me an arrogant stare. "I'm not."

"Whatever you say."

"Cherry."

"Okay, yeah, I need something."

"There it is."

"Alright, you already knew, just shut up about it."

I shrugged, tightening my backpack straps.

"I need you to cover a shift for me," she said, clasping her hands together.

"No."

"What? Why?"

I gave her a look. "You know exactly why."

She crossed her arms, eyebrows furrowed. "You're lazy."

"Okay, yeah, but I've also got plenty of other important stuff I have to do."

"Such as?"

I wouldn't give her the satisfaction, so I said nothing, pressing my lips into a tight line. But also, I had absolutely nothing to do.

She groaned, covering her face with her hands. "It's one day! I have to work on my portfolio!"

There it is. The portfolio card. She wanted to be a designer, someone who made clothes from nothing. She would be perfect at it, and I knew that if she had the time to work on her portfolio, she would get into any school she wanted.

"Please?" she asked, throwing herself forward and wrapping her short arms around me tightly.

"Alright! Fine! I'll cover your shift, just get off me!" I said, pushing her off.

"Yay!" she exclaimed, dancing in a circle and accidentally hitting someone as they walked by. "Oh, sorry!" she called after them, before turning back to me.

I started zoning out as she began telling me about what she was going to put on her portfolio.

Cherry's slivers of deep brown eyes twinkled with excitement as she spoke about her future.

I frowned as I realize for the hundredth time that she was much shorter than I am. I guess her confidence makes her seem much taller than she actually is.

Her short hot pink hair frames her face and bounces as she gestures wildly with ring decorated fingers.

Cherry's family story is actually quite interesting. Cherry was Korean, and she was a third-generation immigrant. Her mom grew up here in Washington and had always strived to prove that their culture in Korea doesn't define Cherry, and she's always been the one adult in my life who has encouraged me to do everything I could to make myself happy. I'm sure Mom would do the same, but she's busy.

Not much could make me super happy anyway. Not with him around. The world is a dangerous place, filled with douchebags like him, and most of it made me so angry that I couldn't feel anything else.

"You get all that?" Cherry asked, her voice bubbling.

"Oh yeah, definitely. Is that jacket new?" I asked, trying to distract her from the fact that I hadn't been listening at all.

She gasped, clutching the sleeves and throwing her head back dramatically. "Why yes, dear friend! I made it a couple days ago!"

Cherry usually makes most of her clothes. She says that she could never find anything that matches her specific style, so she makes them herself. She makes them, like out of fabric and thread! I couldn't even draw a proper stick figure, let alone make my own clothes from nothing.

"It's cool," I told her, grinning.

"Thank you, dear sir," she said, poking me. "Anyway, my shifts on Saturday, and I still have to open the café, so I'm just gonna work on it there," Cherry explained, opening my locker again to snatch a piece of gum. "Just come to my house before and I'll drive you there. Okay?" She slammed my locker shut loudly, and I grumbled under my breath as people around us jumped and turned to glance quickly towards the source of the sound.

The eyes of strangers always made me feel on edge. It's

the way they watch you pass, like you have something wrong with you, or like they need to figure something out about you. It pisses me off for some reason.

"Why don't I just drive myself?"

"Eryn. Do you wanna be paid or not?"

"I have no idea what that has to do with you driving me, but fine," I sighed. "You owe me though."

"I'll buy you an ice cream."

I grinned.

The bell for the first period rang above us, and Cherry started backing away from me as the hallways began to fill up.

"See ya later!" she called before disappearing in the crowd.

"Bye," I said to the empty space in the hallway, sighing as the day began.

Every day begins the same. Wake up, oh hey evil person who couldn't care less about me or my mother, go to school, oh hey people I don't care about, go home, hey again disgustingly horrible guy, sleep. Hello blackness.

I never have dreams. I don't know if that's a bad thing or not, I've heard from a couple people that not having dreams just means I forget them immediately after I wake up, but something about that feels so wrong. Why? Why would not having dreams be a side effect of being tired? I did dream once, a long time ago, back when my mom was happy and my dad was still here. Back when they pretended everything was fine. I used to dream about blue skies and people with bright eyes, a world full of new experiences and opportunities. Once Stepmonster came though, once Mom started carving herself down into a twig of who she once was, nothing came up. Like my brain could not produce anything remotely pleasant at all. Not with him here.

I rubbed my face, blinking as the bell rang loudly again, announcing that once again, I was late. I swore as I hurried away.

I rapped my fist on the large wooden door, chuckling at the muffled yelling.

The outside of Cherry's home was a subdued blue that would've been too much for anyone but them. There were wooden carvings of alligators and cranes sitting in the front garden, surrounded by bright flowers and dogwood trees that bloomed maroon flowers in the spring.

The door opened quickly, and Mrs. Jenkins, Cherry's mom, stuck her head out.

"Eryn! Honey, it's been forever!" she exclaimed, pulling me into a hug.

"Yeah, it feels like forever ago since I last saw you, Mrs. Jenkins." I told her, squeezing her tight.

"Eryn, I've told you a hundred times, call me Marissa," she said, smiling at me warmly. Her hand rubbed my back for a short second before she pulled away, backing away slightly to holding the door for me.

If it was anybody else, anyone in the world, hugging me like that, I would push them away, but there's something about Cherry and Marissa's hugs that made me realize just how touch starved I really am.

"Right, sorry Marissa."

"Come in, come in," she said, ushering me in. "I'm working on something special."

I smiled at the excitement in her voice, knowing that even in the beginning stages of her process, whatever she was making was something she would throw herself into. It's inevitable. It's who she was.

Marissa was someone I knew better than my own mother. Little things, like how at night, if she didn't triple check every lock on the windows and doors, she wouldn't be able to sleep, or the way she drops an extra drop of soy sauce in pretty much everything she makes, and how sometimes when Cherry and I were little, she watched soap operas when we left to go to school.

Marissa also loved woodworking. She whittled and sold her little projects at farmers markets for pocket money, and because of that, she and her house always smelled of wood. I've grown up with the smell clinging to my clothing like sticky sap.

She led me to the corner where her desk was set up, covered in wood shavings and sawdust, grabbing a lump of wood and held it up, smiling like she knew I would adore it.

"What do you think?" she asked, lifting her eyebrows like nothing was more important than hearing my opinion.

I'm gonna be honest: it looks like she made a garbage can, but the enthusiasm in her voice convinced me not to tell her that. I mean, I wouldn't tell that to anyone else. I think.

"Oh!" I exclaimed, squinting my eyes slightly. "Is it… done?"

She smiled and shook her head, making a little noise that sounded like the noise a southern mother would make before saying *isn't he adorable.*

"No! It's gonna be a bear."

I smiled awkwardly. "Yay…"

"It's gonna be you!" Marissa said, hurrying to the stove to stir the fragrant vegetables that I had failed to notice she was cooking.

"But… I'm not a bear?"

"Eryn, honey, I love you like a son, but you're a bit dense. Hungry?" she asked, gesturing towards the food.

"First of all, rude. Second of all, nah, I ate a while ago."

She smiled, reaching for the ladle. My eyes widened at the thought of stuffing my comfortably full stomach with even more food.

I should've guessed she was going to ask me if I was hungry; Korean culture pretty much revolves around food, it was a special way of sharing love that no other culture can replicate in the same way.

She passed me a bowl of rice and vegetables, ruffling my hair lovingly.

"Wait!" she exclaimed, making me jump as she rushed back to the counter, grabbing the soy sauce bottle. She hurried back over, carefully dropping an extra drop or two of soy sauce. "There. Stir it up and chow down."

I nodded, taking a bite. As good as it was, I was already full. This was gonna be painful.

Marissa was very special to me. She raised me when my mom couldn't. I came here at least once a week, and Marissa has always made sure that I was never hungry. Just the smell of her house reminded me of times when Cherry and I had hidden beneath the stairs, covering our mouths as we tried not to sound like we were giggling, but we were, and hysterically at that.

Marissa and Mom, back when they were able to hang out, would giggle too, asking loudly where in the world we could be as they watched us laugh in our favorite place to hide. Despite the weird figurines, she and Cherry were family.

"Is that Eryn?!" Cherry yelled from the top of the stairs. Speak of the devil...

"Yes honey, but give him a minute, he's eating!" She gave me a look. I started wolfing down the food faster than I had already been.

"If you stopped feeding him, we would actually leave early," Cherry called, her voice sounding annoyed.

"Is that an attitude?" Marissa asked, crossing her arms. There was a pause, and Marissa gave me a knowing look as we heard soft footsteps pad down the stairs.

"Can you please let him leave with me?" Cherry asked quietly, now standing in the doorway.

Her small gold earrings made clinking noises as she brushed her straightened hair out of her face. Her dark blue dress swayed as she stepped near me, getting ready to run away.

Marissa nodded. "Yes yes, now get out of here! You'll be late!"

"And who's fault is that?" I mumbled through a mouthful of food, trying to smile when she shot me a look.

"Get out! Bring me coffee when you come home tonight, Cherry!" Marissa yelled after us.

She kissed my cheek as I hurried out the door after Cherry,

cringing at my painfully full stomach.

As we stepped out into the parking lot in front of the café Cherry worked, I held my jacket above my head, jerking my head to Cherry as I gestured to her to share the small space. She ducked under, forced to bend over to fit as the rain pattered against the concrete satisfyingly.

When she reached the back door to the café, she grumbled as she fumbled for her keys. Her grumbling proceeded to get louder as she missed the keyhole, and eventually, the door clicked open under her touch.

She flung open the doors, sighing as she set her large stacks of papers on a nearby table, the loud thud echoing through the dark store.

"I'm back!" she yelled in the empty shop, taking a running leap over the counter and crashing into the wall before heading to the back.

Cherry was the manager of the Rainy Day Café without actually being the manager. She checked stock, got people moving, and opened and closed the place, but if anyone asked for the manager, some other guy came out and talked because Cherry was awful with people.

I wasn't even sure I could even explain just how bad she was with people. There was this one time where she was serving a customer coffee, and he said something about how her apron was all dirty, and she threw the coffee in his face. I laughed for hours afterwards, not being able to shake the image of the guy's shocked face as he started to scream from the burning coffee.

If she wasn't being violent, she just straight up started crying randomly. Someone commented on the rain one day and she just burst into tears, blubbering about how she wasn't going to be able to do anything fun ever with all this rain.

Needless to say, she didn't usually work from the register.

Cherry handed me a green apron that she had just pulled from behind the counter.

"Put in on, big boy," she said, winking at me. I shuddered at her words, backing away from her with my hands up in the air.

"Don't ever say that again, I feel so unbelievably violated," I said, cringing and slipping the apron on. I couldn't help but shudder again as the words echoed through my traumatized brain.

She shrugged, throwing her keys in the air and catching them. She turned to me with an ecstatic look in her easily excited eyes. I rolled my eyes at her, and she smirked, turning back around with an exaggerated hair flip.

She unlocked the front doors, flipping the closed sign to open with an excited wiggle.

"We're open!" she screeched, throwing her arms above her head and doing a little shimmy.

I groaned, banging my head against the wall in mock agony.

She giggled, patting a fellow co-worker on the shoulder affectionately as she headed to the corner of the café.

As I waited for people to arrive, I watched as the sun that had spread weak rays of light this morning disappear behind dark gray clouds, and the bare trees began to shiver in the cold breeze.

After only a couple minutes, the tiny golden bell at the top of the heavy door announced a customer brightly.

She combed the rain from her long blonde hair with her fingers and smiled at me. In any other situation with any other guy, I'm sure they would have described her as an angel, with her blonde hair and pristine tan skin, but I didn't quite notice. I also wasn't attracted to her gender, so that's a pretty big factor I guess.

"Hi!" she breathed, her eyes hungry as they gave me the once over.

"Hello, welcome to the Rainy Day Café, what would you like?" I asked, plastering a smile on my face. I could already tell where this was going to go.

"Clever name," she said, her bright pink lips curling into a simpering smile. "Did you come up with that?"

"Uh... no. I usually don't work here, and I also didn't make the place. What would you like?" I answered after a pause, holding back a sarcastic retort. Do I look like I built the place?

She grinned, giggling at a joke I haven't made.

"Do you want anything?" I asked dryly.

She licked her lips. "What would *you* suggest..." She glanced at my nametag. "Eryn?"

I stared at her blankly for a moment, feeling my chest grow slightly tighter with frustration.

The bell behind her began to ring obsessively as more and more people came in, but she didn't seem to notice, waiting for my answer with an arrogant smile.

"Like I said, I don't usually work here. Order whatever you'd like, but hurry please, there's a line."

She turned to see the line that now reached the door. A couple people shot her annoyed looks as they waited impatiently. I felt a little bad for her, but not bad enough to warrant her arrogant attitude.

"Oh! Wow, I guess this place gets busy!" she exclaimed, turning back to me with pink cheeks.

"Yeah, I'd like to think so. What do you want to get?"

The rest of the day went as smoothly as it could; one or two customers had fits about their orders being too warm, not enough sugar, but that's a given in this line of work.

Eventually, my break rolled around, and I waved to Cherry.

The massive pile of papers had been spread all around her, and she had moved from the table to the floor. Customers sat and talked around her quietly, giving her a wide radius of space. She mumbled to herself as she moved glossy pictures of full dresses and outfits she had created. She glanced up, her brow furrowed before breaking into a smile.

She waved back, pulling her hair into a ponytail as she continued to attack the slowly dwindling stack of papers beside her.

I left the register, clapping a different employee on the shoulder as I headed to the back room.

I found a quiet space in the storage room, and, sitting on a box that *wouldn't* collapse this time, I started eating the granola bar Cherry had slipped me earlier today.

It was terrible, really. And by that, I meant it was stale, and it was some whole grain bar thing, and the blueberries were mushy.

However, it was food, the only food I had today, so I consumed the monstrosity despite the fruit.

The soft sounds of clinking glass and murmuring voices filled the back. The small room was filled with the smell of coffee and chocolate. It made the granola bar taste better, which was fantastic, because it really wasn't good at all.

I took a deep breath and leaned against the wall, feeling sleepy.

Every foot of this place reminded me of the past. Cherry's been working here since sophomore year of high school, so she's been dragging me here to cover her shifts for years. Usually, she actually works, but there have been a couple times that she dragged me here under the false pretenses of working together and ditched me for some guy. She always returned an hour later, feeling so guilty for leaving me here that she would apologize for hours after I had already forgiven her.

It's not that I don't enjoy being at the café, it's just that I'm here all the time after school and on the weekends. It was fine, I don't have anywhere else to go, but just like Cherry, I'm not that great with people. I mean, I don't start crying, but they affect me. They annoy me, lighting the flame of anger in my chest.

I tried not to be, but life moves on without me. I don't have control over that part of myself. I just have to live with it, even if I am angry every day of my god-forsaken life.

Sometimes, when I sat at the register, ringing people up for their daily dose of caffeine, I wondered if anyone would actually remember me. If I would pass that person the next day and have no idea who they were. Maybe they would remember me, but I wouldn't know who they were. It's a strange thought to have on a Saturday afternoon, to realize that I have participated in hundreds of thousands of people's lives without knowing a single detail about them.

Did that mean my existence is futile? If not even one remembers me? I shook my head. No, of course not. Everyone had a purpose. Even me.

I've been sitting for too long. My thighs ached as I struggled to right myself over the crushed box.

"Hey!" The door suddenly slammed open, sending me to my feet, and the taste of metal filled my mouth as I bit my tongue in a sudden rush of fear.

"*Alright, what?!*" I yelled at Cherry, who was pressing her lips tightly together, trying not to laugh. I stood up, grunting as the pressure was released in my muscles. I clenched my fists as I glared at her.

"You gotta get back to work," she said, wiping her eyes. "We don't get long breaks, sorry."

"Don't 'sorry' me," I grumbled, pushing past her, deeply annoyed that she had interrupted my train of thought.

I grind my teeth together when I heard her burst into laughter as I turned the corner.

I've never been able to intimidate her, which was so unbelievably annoying. Everyone else crosses sides when I walked down streets, and here comes my best friend, someone who crosses the street to get to me.

I stepped up to the register once more, now frustrated to my core.

The day dragged by slowly as I watched as people talk, laughing and tracking mud in from the rainy weather outside.

The day was now slower than I had ever imagined a day could be.

A small trickle of people walking in every once in a while, the bell alerting me of their presence each time, never failing to emit its cheerful ring, and God, I hated that bell.

The day had been relatively nice, but now the rain began to fall quicker than it had been forecasted, the clouds heavy and dark with drops of water. I watched the rain make tracks down the windows, gritting my teeth as a group of people laughed loudly.

The windows fogged up slightly as the heat from the moving bodies inside met the cold from outside in a war of steam, and customers' wet shoes made the floor squeak.

I narrowed my eyes at the hunched figure outside. They were fidgeting slightly, pacing back and forth in front of the door.

I couldn't see their face, I couldn't even tell how tall they were through the foggy windows, but I was suspicious. I also didn't want to go check, knowing that I would be drenched the second I step outside I got out there to see what's up.

The door creaked open, and a sudden gust of wind practically pushed the small hunched figure standing outside in.

They stood there for a moment, surveying the area from under their large hood that covered their face. The figure squeezed one of their blue sleeves carefully after a moment, and a stream of water hit their shoe. I mentally groan, knowing that it would be extra time here to mop it. I was making Cherry clean that up.

I could hear their sigh from the counter. I bit back an amused smile, knowing how awful the feeling of wet socks in shoes was.

The figure shuffled over to the register, pulling their wet hood off, and—

"Hi," he said, pushing his drenched hair out of his face. His voice sounded shaky and nervous, but it was smooth, and so quiet that I could barely hear him. I wanted to listen to him forever. "I've never been to this coffee place before, what would you suggest?"

Usually, when customers ask me that, I had to force myself to smile and suggest whatever my eyes landed on first, but with him, I felt like I would tell him anything he asked. If he asked me to give him my car, I would say yes, I swear to God, I would say yes.

His hair was lit up from behind, and it looked like gold as he stood in front of me, brighter than anything I had ever been lucky enough to see.

I could barely hear him through the fog that gathered in my brain. I felt like I had been hit with a truck.

His blue eyes kept glancing at me, then somewhere else; an urge in my chest swelled to catch his attention and keep it.

"Uh, I would suggest the... er..." I tore my eyes away to glance at the board behind me. I had to find something good, something that would make him remember me. "Hot chocolate. Or anything chocolate really. Perfect with the rainy weather."

He smiled, and my heart leaped into my throat. I found myself actually smiling back.

"Okay, chocolate it is. I'll have a mocha and a chocolate chip cookie please."

I rang him up, sneaking glances at him.

He was tall enough to reach my shoulders, and his wet jacket clung to his broad shoulders and chest. His cheeks turned pink, making the freckles stand out against the blush that was spreading over his nose.

I felt lightheaded.

Was I getting sick? I pressed my hand to my forehead quickly, not feeling any difference in temperature as my arm. No fever. Maybe it was him?

His eyes looked back up at me, and I felt my eyes lock onto his, my head feeling like I was floating for a moment before I moved quickly, grabbing for anything physical on the counter before me. Yep. Definitely him.

"Name?" I asked, seizing a pen and a sticky note.

"Parker."

chapter two
try chocolate

Parker

"Parker," I told him, trying to ignore my burning cheeks. "Hey, um, am I allowed to use that library over there?" I pointed to the small shelf of books by a squashy armchair in the corner of the café.

An uncomfortable feeling washed over me as I realized how terrifyingly intimidating he looked, what with his hair covering his entire forehead and his eyes ever so slightly narrowed as he watched me.

Do I leave? No no, I've already ordered something, might as well stay now. What's the worst that could happen?

The barista looked at me curiously, his lips curling into a small amused smile. "Of course." His voice was deeper than I'd thought when I had first seen him.

"Thanks." I quickly made my way to the armchair to claim the spot, hoping he wasn't judging me as I clutched my sleeves in my grasp and large drops of water fell on the shiny floor.

I shed my wet hoodie and sighed at the unpleasant

feeling of my shirt sticking to my skin, my shoes squeaking as I turned to sit in the chair.

It cradled my weight, and I shook my head, picking out an interesting looking book.

I wasn't planning on going home anytime soon. After all, Father isn't exactly the nicest man in the world.

Don't get me wrong, my mom has always been there. She used to tell me she loved me all the time, she always fed me every night, and she did raise me from a baby, but the way she speaks to me wasn't the same as it once was.

Today was their anniversary, so I couldn't be there—they didn't want me to be anywhere near home. That's fine though, I was used to it. I was usually an unwanted presence in a room.

Earlier today, when I had come home from the secluded bookstore in town, the back door was locked. There was no note, no indication that they were even there.

I dropped my stuff by the door and left, knowing it was locked for a reason.

Glimpses of my own blond hair and too-big shoulders I caught in shop windows had been making me anxious despite the hoodie drawn tight over my face, so I ducked into the first door I found.

Now, I couldn't stop staring at the barista.

As scary as he seemed, he was also so hot that it was almost unfair. He was almost a head taller than me, and while I had been standing directly in front of him, I couldn't help but wonder how tall he really was.

His dark hair was swept up in the front, like he ran his fingers through it all the time, and his full eyebrows were furrowed as he answered a new customer's question.

I shivered, half from the cold, half from nerves.

He doesn't seem so scary after all. Not with the way he smiled at a girl with pink hair as she came out from the back, patting his back as she said something to him. He laughed, nodding as she grinned and sat heavily down at another armchair that was across the room from mine.

Bella Van Winkle

I desperately wanted to talk to him, to tell him everything I knew about this world we lived in and everything I wished I would be able to love, but I couldn't. I just couldn't, I didn't trust the way words fell from my lips.

He wouldn't like the way they sounded. Would he? No, of course not. He couldn't.

I didn't even know his name, but the way he made me feel from only a couple sentences was terrifying.

A while ago, about a year ago, when I first came out to my parents, they were both mortified. Father threatened to tell my teachers and everyone I knew, so I've tried to keep myself under control, and I've been pretty successful, at least to my standards. Father's standards were much different.

But now, watching the way the barista's lips formed sickly sweet sentences that he passed on to customers, I knew this was going to be a massive problem.

I flipped through the pages of my book, trying to force my racing mind to stop thinking about him, but I couldn't get his stupefied smile out of my head.

The look he gave me when I walked in made me feel like I was the most amazing thing he'd ever seen.

Now, he looked like he hated being here, but when he caught my gaze, he grinned.

I quickly stared down at my book again, blushing furiously.

Should I ask him something? What would I even ask, I didn't have any questions, other than the obvious can I have your number question, but I was not going to ask him, I'd rather die—

"Parker?" I jumped, fumbling with my book at the sudden voice. I ruffled my hair as I glanced up, hoping they wouldn't notice my blush.

The barista stood over me with a steaming mug, a cookie, and an amused smile. How did he get over here so quickly?

"Sorry," I mumbled, continuing to run my fingers through my hair nervously. "I was zoning out, I guess."

He chuckled. "Yeah, I could see that. I take it you're

staying?" he asked, his voice hopeful.

"Ye-yeah, I am," I replied, rubbing my arms.

"Good. It's getting bad out there, and besides, it's nice to have someone like you in here. It's refreshing," he said, setting my order on the small table beside me. He stepped slightly closer to my chair, sending the scent of chocolate and coffee wafting towards me. It was heavenly.

"Someone like me?" I asked, feeling flustered.

"Yeah. Cute."

Oh. *Oh.* My face burst into flames and I sputtered, looking anywhere but him.

He was lying, lying to make me feel better, and I hated his pity, as nice as it was to hear.

He smiled at me, either not noticing my embarrassment or ignoring it.

"Let me know if you need anything. My name is Eryn."

Eryn walked back behind the counter and disappeared into the back.

I let out a breath I didn't realize I'd been holding and slumped back into my chair, rubbing my face.

I stared at the ceiling, replaying the entire encounter, regretting most of it. I heard Eryn's deep voice telling me his name on repeat, over and over. Unfortunately, this made my cheeks even warmer.

He looked so threatening though, the sliver of a scar through his eyebrow making him look like he could beat me up in a second and I wouldn't even have time to blink. But his eyes... the warmth his eyes seemed to produce made me believe that he would never do that to me.

I glanced back at the counter.

Instead of Eryn, there was the girl with pink hair I had seen earlier, watching me intensely, her chin propped up on her hand. There was a scary grin on her face, like she was planning something.

I quickly looked away, my heart beating fast.

Maybe she's mad because of my encounter with her... boyfriend? Oh great, was Eryn her boyfriend?

I mentally groaned. I'm just the right person to throw this divebomb at, right Universe?

I went back to the paragraph I've been trying to read since I walked in, but embarrassment and self-pity made the book unbearably boring.

"So." I jumped again, dropping my book and somehow smacking myself in the face.

"Oh! Oh my gosh, are you okay? I didn't mean to scare you, I'm so sorry!" the pink-haired girl said, grabbing my hand and lightly tapping the side of my nose.

"No, it's fine, it's not the first time that's happened today," I said, horrified at this entire situation and hoping this would end soon, whatever *this* was about to be.

"Yeah, I noticed earlier. You're fine," she said, dropping my hand and straightening back up.

I stayed quiet, praying she would leave.

Her deep brown eyes narrowed as she gave me the once over, and I suddenly wanted to crawl into a hole.

"Do you... need anything?" I asked after a moment of silence, rubbing my hands together.

"Oh yeah!" Her face lit up. "So I saw you watching my friend. He brought you your order, right?" I nodded warily. "Good, cool, cause that's my best friend and he's desperate for love." She smiled, like I had an idea where this conversation was going.

"Listen, I know that I don't know you and you definitely don't know me," she said, wincing slightly at that. "My best friend is that guy over there, Eryn Harper, who you met." She points to the hot guy behind the counter who was currently handing a man his coffee, a mischievous smirk languidly spread across his face as if he spit in that guy's drink. It made butterflies explode in my stomach, and suddenly I yearned to be near him, to be laughing with him, to be the reason he was smiling.

"He's so hopeless when he looks for guys," she continued. I hadn't realized she was still talking. "He was checking you out too, so..." She flipped her hair over her shoulder casually.

"What?"

"You're a great choice, I'm glad you showed up."

I sputtered, choking on my drink. "No, I mean... what?" Good choice for what? Is that all I was? A good enough choice?

She leaned in uncomfortably close. "Date my friend."

"I don't know either of you! Who are you?" I asked loudly, standing up suddenly. I looked up, suddenly realizing that more than one group of people were watching me cautiously, and I quickly sat back down, my cheeks hot. God, I hoped he didn't notice.

"Oh right, silly me," she said, hitting her forehead. "Cherry Jesperson at your service. And you are?" She stuck her hand out, smiling as she waited for my answer.

"Parker," I told her, shaking her hand.

"Last name?"

"Last names aren't important."

"They are too!" Cherry said with a mock gasp.

"Not for me. Please, just drop it." Last names will never be important to me. Not while Father still had the same last name as me. Not when I've tarnished the family name with my own disgusting thoughts, thick like black paint.

"Fine, but I'll wrangle it out of you one day!" she told me, grinning now.

I smiled, somehow feeling a bit more at ease.

"So. The date?" Cherry asked hopefully.

"Oh, um... I guess if he wants to, I suppose I will." She screeched in happiness. "But I just..." I trailed off, taking a sip of my now cold coffee. How long had she been talking to me? How could this be cold already?

She tilted her head, standing up and adjusting her belt over her dark green dress. "Don't worry, he already likes you, you'll be fine."

"Yeah, okay," I answered, rolling my eyes. Like anyone could ever like me.

She winked and practically fell over her forgotten chair in her haste to retrieve Eryn.

I tried to get back to my book, but my body was wracked with nerves as I waited for his approval, so I finally set it down.

This was a terrible idea, how could I ever agree to this, I knew very well just how disgusting my preference for guys is, Father has made sure of it. This was a horrible idea. What about Cherry made me feel safe enough to say yes to this?

I chewed my nails as I waited, knowing that whatever was about to happen would be disastrous, but I also didn't want to leave—I couldn't—not when there was a chance that he would speak to me. And Cherry was so very convinced that this was a surefire way of forcing us together.

Forcing us together. That's all this is, and when has forcing people together ever gone right?

I kicked off my still soggy shoes and pulled my knees to my chest, fluffing my hair nervously. The anticipation was killing me. I reached for my drink, knowing it was cold but needing a distraction.

As bad as I felt about this whole idea, something gnawed at me. Maybe this wouldn't be so bad.

I've never had a boyfriend before, not even a girlfriend, back when I thought liking girls was the only option. I've never felt the urge to. Most of the guys in school were jerks, making jokes about queers. None of them had ever caught my attention. I mostly tried to avoid *their* attention.

But there was something about Eryn, something in his eyes that made me want to listen. When he looked at me, he saw me, he stared into my eyes like I was the only thing he wanted to see.

A warm hand on my shoulder jolted me out of my churning thoughts, and I looked up to see Eryn holding a fresh cup of coffee.

"Hi." He grinned, handing me the cup.

"H-hi." I held it close to my cold face. It was so *warm*, but it didn't smell like the mocha I had ordered before. "From Cherry?"

He nodded, a small smile on his lips. "She said you needed something stronger than a mocha. I hope you like two sugars and cream in your coffee, 'cause that's what I put in it."

"Yeah, that's fine." I laughed awkwardly, feeling my face grow warm again. At least I wasn't cold anymore. "So she told you about the uh, idea?"

"She did," he replied, pulling a chair over and sitting in front of me, adjusting his black T-shirt, his apron now gone. He didn't look annoyed to be here, like I thought he would be

Maybe he was good at hiding it?

"Are you done for today?" I took a sip and shivered at the warmth suddenly spreading through my apparently still cold body. I need dry clothes.

"Yeah, I got off a couple of minutes ago."

I nodded, watching him carefully, worried he would ask me something personal. That's not what this is for, I didn't need personal, and I couldn't need anything like him, but this was something I wasn't used to. I didn't know how this worked.

Neither of us said anything. Eryn watched me with his ever-present confident smile.

His eyes were so expressive that I felt like I could fall into the deepest brown I had ever seen and feel more than I had ever felt. I couldn't tear my gaze away despite my overwhelming embarrassment.

"Tell me something about you," he said, leaning forward.

"Already?" I asked, gripping my cup tighter.

"I don't know you, as much as I want to, it's kinda weird to go out with a stranger, right?"

"I guess," I responded, feeling flustered from his sly compliment. "What do you wanna know?"

"Anything."

Anything. That's a big word, wasn't it? Anything and everything. I wanted to tell him that was a horrible answer, to tell me to talk about something that was more important to me, to the world, something I believed in, but I didn't know what made the world better. I didn't know what I believed in anymore, but if even if I did, I wished he would ask me about it.

I slid my feet back on the floor, trying to think of something that wouldn't disgust him.

"Well, I uh, I'm—" I stopped, taking a deep breath to try again. "I like reading."

Eryn smiled softly. Damn my racing heart.

"Why?" he asked, running his hands through his dark hair. "I'm not really one for reading, I get bored really easily."

Interesting. "It's nice. Takes my mind off things. It's like going to a whole world without ever standing up, and usually, I'd rather be anywhere than... uh, here I guess." I shouldn't have said anything at all.

"I like that. That's a good way to think."

"Yeah, I guess so." My heart raced. What was I supposed to say to him?

"What part of here do you not want to be in?" His eyes weren't unkind as he watched me, but the way the words fell from his lips set me on edge.

"I uh... all of it, I guess."

"Hmm."

Eryn's hands rubbed together, and out of the corner of my eyes, I could see Cherry watching us like a hawk, her eyes narrowed as she tried to read our lips, but Eryn never once broke eyes contact with me.

We were quiet. I picked at my nails, hoping I wouldn't have to break the fragile feeling silence. I ruined this, didn't I?

When I looked up, he was still staring at me. I don't recognize the look in his eyes. Kindness perhaps? Impressed? What, with me?

There was nothing impressive about me. Nothing at all.

At that unexpected thought, my face was hotter than ever. I had to leave.

I gulped my coffee down, burning my throat and stood up, wincing at the squelch my shoes made as I slipped them on.

"Leaving already?" Eryn asked, standing up as quickly as I had. Why did he care?

"Yeah, I have to... yeah," I answered pathetically.

Eryn cocked his head, watching me hopefully. He'd eventually be disappointed with me.

"Will I see you again?" He asked.

"I don't know..."

"Please? We could go to a movie, maybe dinner?" Despite everything that had flown through my head in the short period of time that I've known Eryn, my stomach filled with butterflies. It was a different type of flight, but it was enough for me to make my mind up.

"I uh, I—" I rubbed the back of my neck. "Yeah. Sure."

Grinning, he stepped forward, giving me a hug. I was shocked into silence as I discovered that his arms reached all the way around me. His arms felt strong, and I let a comfortable feeling wash over me for a split second. My own arms couldn't wrap around him, but God, I didn't realize how touch starved I was.

He stepped away all too quickly, shoving his hands into his pockets as he glanced quickly behind him at Cherry, who shot him a thumbs up.

He had a small silver scar on his jawline, and it seemed more real than anything I've ever believed in.

Time seemed to slow for us as we watched each other, small smiles moving our lips.

"Well... bye," I whispered.

"Bye."

I grabbed my jacket and struggled to get into it as the damp cloth dragged against my now dry shirt, blushing sheepishly as Eryn chuckled at my struggles.

Picking up the book I had been trying to read and putting it away, I shuffled away slowly, knowing he was watching me as I did. I waved as I stepped out of the café, back into the cold rain and strong winds, away from warmth and coffee and a waving boy with kind eyes.

It seemed like the wind was pushing me farther away from the coffee shop, the rain biting my skin with frozen teeth. Dark clouds covered the sky in harsh waves, only allowing the slightest bit of light through.

My body was already shaking from the icy rain sinking through my already damp jacket, and I shivered from the cold that began seeping into my bones once more.

A wave of water practically drowned me as a car drove by through a puddle, the headlights reflecting off the water into my eyes, blinding me for a split second. I sputtered, stumbling back. A gust of wind shoved me hard over a bush and into a ditch that was filled with an inch of rainwater, and I gasped as the cold spread over my head and back.

Pain shot through my body, forcing the breath from my lungs.

I didn't want to move. I couldn't go back to the café, there was no way that anyone would have seen me, and even if they did, I wouldn't want them to help me anyway. Can't go home either, Father has made that very clear.

Does anyone want me? The only people who are expected to love me don't, so what's the point? I'm just a waste of food. Of air. Water. Time.

The rain stung my open eyes, but I didn't care enough to close them; the very thought of closing my eyes to protect them from the rain that pelted down was too exhausting to imagine.

In the dim light that the skies provided, I had to squint to see the scars on my wet arms. It's not serious. I told myself every day for as long I could remember that it wasn't an actual issue, it was just a way to control something when I couldn't control anything else, and that was the truth. At least for a while. This is all I have left, I suppose.

I hate the scars. They'll be there forever, and it's so much work to hide the more recent ones, and the looks, the stares when I wore a T-shirt was too much to bear.

I let my arm fall over my eyes, not caring enough to get up, the energy leaving my body and mind as quickly as it had come.

Will Eryn like me? Does he? Of course not, that's not possible.

This is stupid. The idea that this one guy, in the five

minutes that I had known him, could kickstart all these ridiculous thoughts in my head.

I sighed, rain dripping off the sides of my face as I finally blinked.

I knew I should've gotten up, I should be making my way home, to my room and bed, but I didn't. I couldn't find the energy to force myself up. What was the point? It wasn't as if anyone was waiting for me at home, or if anyone would worry about where I was.

I wondered if I should stay here, wait until someone did find me.

I sighed again, barely being able to find the energy to do as simple of a thing as breathing.

Not yet. Not today.

chapter three
you're blue against a world of grey

I couldn't stop smiling. His words bounced around my head like balloons, his quiet laughter when I gave him his coffee.

Seeing Cherry come crashing into the back room when I was grabbing more coffee beans for a coworker who was too busy to leave his station was shocking, to say the least. She was so excited, her eyes wild and her face red, and she had been spouting random words like 'go', and 'a date'. When I asked her what was happening, all she said was that Parker, the guy she saw me watching was waiting for me.

I had stood there for a moment, trying to put together her random words. When I finally did, a smile grew on my face, and a warm feeling spread over my chest. She'd laughed when I tore off the apron and threw it under the counter. She'd told me to get him stronger coffee for him, and I hastily complied, whipping up a black coffee and taking a deep breath before heading out to talk to him.

He had been so jumpy, chewing on his nails like he clung to the feeling of his teeth scraping his nails to stop himself from leaving. And when I asked him what he liked to do...

God, the light that popped into his eyes was amazing, I couldn't stop staring.

For the first time in a long time, I was excited for tomorrow. I didn't care about those people who had been watching us talk, I didn't feel an ounce of anger when I spotted Cherry trying to figure out what we were saying. All I cared about was that tomorrow, I was going to find him, and I was going to talk to him.

"You done for the day?" Cherry asked, hopping up onto the counter, breaking my train of thought.

"Yeah. You?"

She nodded, taking the folded apron I had stashed behind the counter and chucked it into the back room. I snorted when it hit a half-empty bag of coffee, sending it tumbling to the floor.

"Can I take your car home? I gotta go home to Mom soon, you know, make sure she's okay."

"Yeah," she said, tossing me the keys. "I'll just ask one of my other friends for a ride, I gotta clean up. Tell Tammy I said hi."

She always said that, every time I mention Mom. I could never express to her how much that means, when I haven't heard anyone say her name gently like that in a while.

"I will. See ya," I said, grinning at Cherry's exuberant waving. "Oh yeah." I paused, looking back at her. "I just wanted to say uh… thanks." My voice was much quieter than I had meant it to be.

"Anytime. You were desperate anyway," she said, a smug expression on her face, but I knew that she was happy about my success, as small as it was.

"Shut up," I stuck my tongue out at her before heading out of the Rainy Day Café and into the rain darkened clouds, a small smile stuck on my face.

Raindrops splattered across the dashboard as I launched myself into Cherry's car, trying to get in before I got soaked.

Sighing, I turned the key and started to drive out of the parking lot. The sky was much darker than it had been when

Cherry and I arrived here, but the bare trees were still stark against the dark sky. The road was shiny with rain, the headlights of Cherry's car making the road look as though it was made of glass.

I sat in silence, thinking about the day and what I still had to do when I got home. I never really turned on the radio, most of the songs made my crowded mind fuzzy. Even without music, I felt like my brain was full to bursting.

Speaking of full to bursting, Parker was... he was amazing. I barely talked to him, barely knew what his voice sounded like when he talked about things he loved, but he was so different than anyone I have ever met.

I heard so much resistance and fear in his voice; they laced every word he uttered. I had a strange urge to smooth them out, to guide him through our words until he sounded excited and passionate.

Not only that, but he didn't make me feel angry, he didn't light anything in my chest but interest. That couldn't be a coincidence, not when everyone else sends me into blazes.

I sighed, my throat suddenly feeling tight. This was weird. I was too eager, wasn't I? Maybe he hadn't been nervous because of the situation, but because I was too forward.

I shook my head, trying to shake away those unwanted thoughts. Despite everything, I wanted to see him again.

I glanced out my window as I slowed on the slick road, sighing heavily. My eyes caught a glimpse of sky blue, and I squinted, trying to see better through the rain.

No. Was that—?

I gasped at the flash of a blue sweatshirt and slammed on the brakes, pulling over as quickly as I could.

Parker.

In the back of my mind, I wondered how I was able to see him from behind the large hedge that grew in front of his drenched form as I scrambled out of my car, rushing towards Parker's drenched body.

I slid to my knees as I neared his body, pulling Parker towards me.

"Parker? Oh, come on, I just met you! Wake up! Parker?"

He blinked his eyes open and squinted at me. "Oh. Hi Eryn."

"Thank god. What's wrong with you? I thought you were dead! Get up, let's go," I groaned, starting to help him up. "Did you pass out? How did you get there?"

"I didn't pass out, I was just… sitting for a bit," he replied, making no effort to help me as I pulled him up from the filthy puddle he had been lying in.

"What, in the pouring rain? Are you insane?"

"Could be."

"That is so not funny, I'm bringing you somewhere warm," I told him, trying to drag him to my car as he began to help me by standing.

"Why? Where are we going?"

His feet suddenly slipped from underneath him, and I rushed to catch him, my heart dropping as I did.

My own feet slid in the mud as I slipped my arms under his, struggling to hold him up as he tried to steady his slightly shaking legs.

"Sorry, I—" Parker stopped talking abruptly.

I looked up to see Parker's face inches from my own, rain sliding down his pink cheeks like tears.

His wide eyes were much bluer than I had thought.

"I um… sorry," Parker mumbled, his cheeks turning an even darker pink.

"It's okay." I blinked, shaking my head slightly to clear the sudden fog in my head. "Here, I'll uh, help you." I slung one of his arms over my shoulders and helped him to the car.

"Hey, you good?" I asked, noticing a limp as he walked with me, his eyes focused on the ground.

"Yeah, I'm fine," he said, shaking his head as his feet slid in the mud again. I'm not sure if I believed him, but I didn't say anything else, knowing that he would probably get upset if I did.

I let him get into my car by himself, not wanting to hover around him, but I closed his door behind him before making my way to the driver's side.

"Okay?" I looked over to see Parker twisting his hands nervously.

"Yeah." We sat in silence for a moment.

"Alright! Let's go!" I said loudly. "Where do you live?"

"No," he answered, his face still pink from the cold. "I don't want to go home yet, I mean."

"Sure," I tried to answer nonchalantly, ignoring the butterflies. This was sooner than I'd thought I'd get to see him again. "Let's go to the… library."

He snorted. "Do you even read?"

I snorted, trying to make him laugh. "Look at me, Parker. Don't I look like a sophisticated reader?" He gave me a disbelieving look, his eyes bright as he bit his lip. "Doesn't matter! I'm already driving!"

We arrived at the library in silence, the pounding rain the only thing that kept us grounded. We're both so awkward around each other that I'm worried we won't ever be able to able to talk, but even if he doesn't, I will. I will know him eventually.

Parker smiled nervously as he got out, looking at me questioningly.

I gestured towards the library grandly. His cheeks turned red once more. A drop of rain slid down his forehead from under his hair that plastered to his forehead, and I reached out, flicking it away with my thumb wordlessly. I didn't miss his flinch.

We walked up together, our feet pounding in sync, and the swarm of thoughts proceeded to disappear when I held the door open for him, and he smiled at me. I wanted so badly to hold his hand.

Parker looked much calmer the moment the quiet sound of rustling papers reached us. He took a deep breath and his brow creases lessened, and I was fascinated by that change.

He immediately found the fiction section and started searching. I tried to find a book too, but I kept getting distracted. By him.

His hair fell over his eyes as he read the back of books quickly, his lips pursed as he concentrated. I pretended to read the backs of books, but eventually I decided not to get one, that I was fine just sitting.

Occasionally, he would glance up at me like he was afraid I would leave. There was no chance of that.

I found myself completely content watching him, like nothing was going on in my life, no Stepmonster, nothing important happening. I was able to sit down and relax for a moment.

After he found a book and sat down, it was like he forgot I was there. I didn't mind, it was easier to think from the chair in front of him.

He had freckles, I noticed with a smile.

I should be getting home to Mom. I really should be doing homework, or trying to get Stepmonster out of the house so Mom could have some time to heal from everything he had done, so why does this feel more important? Obviously, it wasn't, it's just one guy in a world of guys, but this one wasn't just a guy, and I don't know why. I had to find out why he wasn't like everyone else.

"Excuse me?" I blinked, looking up at the smiling woman beside me.

"Yes?"

She gestured for me to come over, to which I begrudgingly complied, grinning at Parker when he looked up cautiously.

She waited for me with a polite kindness, a look that made me angry.

When I reached the woman, her expression fell, making me immediately on edge. She wasn't here to talk about the weather.

"Is he alright?" she asked, pointing at Parker with an annoyingly nasally voice. I watched as his face turned bright red, and he hastily stared down at his book once more. How dare she. How dare she make him feel less than.

"Yeah, of course. Why wouldn't he be?" I asked,

frustration lacing every word.

"It's just that you're staring at him."

"Oh no, I didn't realize I was, he's just my—" I stopped, looking closely at her, then at Parker. "Yeah. He's fine."

She smiled, her concerned lessened I suppose, and walked away without another word, and I made my way back to my seat, staring at the floor.

I shouldn't have to feel like this. There shouldn't be people like her who feel like they have a reason to stop us from living. He was a good person from what I knew about him already, and I wanted to be with him the moment he opened up. I don't think he ever will if they unknowingly force him to feel like he isn't enough. Everyone is enough for themselves. So is he. How can I convince him of that?

"Eryn?" I looked up. "Is everything okay?" His eyes were narrowed, a concerned expression on his pink face.

I plastered on a smile, a strange tight feeling in my chest. "Yeah. Everything is cool."

We stayed at the library for almost three hours, and as much as I like Parker, I faded in and out of sleep.

I dreamt of blue eyes drowning in the deepest water I had ever seen. I eventually woke up after I had a small pile of paper balls and erasers on my lap.

I snorted at Parker's closed eye in the attempts of throwing another eraser at me again.

"Parker."

"Hmm?"

"I'm *hella* bored."

"Alright."

"So…"

He chuckled when the eraser he had carefully aimed with hit my shoulder.

"So who are you?" I asked, leaning forward, sending the small mountain of paper and eraser pieces cascading to the ground.

"What?" Parker looked apprehensive, his fingers flipping through his book's pages, his eyes watching mine.

"What makes you... you?" I felt awkward. This was such a weird way to start a conversation.

"That's um... that's a very broad question," he said, closing the book. His brows were furrowed, but he hadn't stopped the conversation yet. That must mean something at least.

"Sorry um how about..." I chuckled. "What were you doing out there?"

"Out where?" His face looked innocent of his crimes, but there was a swipe of mud under his ear, and his whole back was dried in ripples of muddy water.

"In the rain. The puddle? Remember that?" I teased.

"Oh. Right." Something about the way his voice dropped to a mumble made me feel uneasy. "I um," he started, looking back down at his hands. "I tripped. Fell backwards and landed in that puddle."

"And?"

"And what?"

"Why did you stay there?"

He shrugged. "Couldn't find the energy."

"You felt really cold," I told him, watching for his reaction. "When I helped you up."

"It *was* cold, I guess." I threw my hands up, pulling my chair closer to him. "It's forty degrees outside!"

He shrugged again. Alright.

"Okay fine, but you scared the crap out of me. You should feel bad," I said deciding to drop the subject. "What's your favorite movie?"

"My favorite... why?" He narrowed his eyes at me.

"I just wanna know our similarities," I stage-whispered, a grin slowly growing on my cheeks. "Is that bad? I could ask something else, if you want me to."

"No, no, it's fine. Um, I like superhero movies," he said, and I watched as his cheeks turned pink. "And I uh... I like romantic movies."

"What a surprise!" His head shot up, his eyes wild with panic. "I love those genres too." I finished, softening my voice.

He nodded, looking around and leaving us in uncomfortable silence.

"But why?" I asked, pretending to think; tapping my hand on my chin. "The mouse likes romance?"

"I uh," Parker coughs, his face bright red. "They have happy endings. I like that."

"Really?" Somehow, somehow, that didn't surprise me. "Cool."

I wanted him to ask me why I loved them, and I wanted to tell him because, in romance, people found out who they were together, because they end up not alone. Something about that fascinated me. I have no idea why, but it did. The way they were able to be hot messes in the beginning of the movie, the cheesy ones, and then end up happy. Happy and with someone they once couldn't stand, or they never thought they'd have a chance with.

But he didn't. He just watched me with his blue eyes, smiling slightly like he knew exactly why.

And I wasn't angry. I wasn't, not at all. It was something about him, the way he was quiet and I still knew what he was thinking without knowing him at all.

So I smiled back.

"Ask me a question." He raised his eyebrows a little. "Ask me something."

"Oh um..." He was quiet, looking at the ceiling above us for a moment. "Why were you so nice to me and not to the other customers?"

"Whoa, was I—" I started, but he waved his hands frantically, cutting me off.

"I just meant because you were so nice to me and when I went back to my seat your smile didn't reach your eyes anymore," he said in one breath, blinking hard.

"I... I didn't realize I was doing that," I started, rubbing the back of my neck.

If I dumped all my issues on him now, there was a massive possibility that he would leave right now. Then again, he was the one that asked me, and all I wanted to do was tell him the truth.

"I have this issue... I guess." I hope this wouldn't make him leave. "My dad was really angry all the time, and basically taught me to um, respond to most situations with anger too."

He was quiet for a moment before saying, "Have you gone to a therapist?"

"Yeah actually," I responded, laughing awkwardly to relieve tension. "They said I had anger issues, and I already kinda knew, so it wasn't all that helpful."

"Is it better now? Easier to manage?"

I sighed, leaning back and crossing my arms. "I think so. It's not gone, but I try not to give in to it."

Parker nodded, watching me carefully.

"But I would never hurt you, I'm not dangerous," I said, sitting up straight. "I promise."

He smiled, and my head spun as he said, "I didn't think you would."

His eyes glittered, and I saw myself in them.

"So... is your dad still around?" Parker asked, picking at his nails.

"Nope. Long gone." I had nothing else *to* say.

"Do you miss him?"

And that is what made me pause. There was something there, something in his voice that sounded both hopeful and unbelievably lonely. I wanted to fix that, I wanted to make that lonely go away.

"No. I don't," I told him, resting my elbows on my knees. "He left a long time ago, and he made my mom miserable. I didn't miss him then, and I don't miss him know."

He nodded. Something fell behind his eyes, and we listened to the rain pound onto the glass ceilings of the dim library.

"What's *your* dad like?" I asked.

He looked down, his curly hair falling in front of his eyes. "He's uh... loud. Angry. Like yours, I guess."

My dad used to yell at my mom until her voice was

drowned out. My ears ring when it's too quiet, because he used to yell at everything that changed.

Until I was in fourth grade, I had no idea that Dads weren't supposed to yell like that. Once I found out, Mom divorced him, and he was gone. I haven't seen him since.

He used to come to my soccer games when I was a kid. He screamed at me while I played, and there was a dad of one of the other kids who would come up to me ask how my mom was. Every time my dad saw him, he would tear me away, shouting that I was being disrespectful and I remember yelling back that I had done nothing wrong.

He'd slapped the side of my head so hard I saw white, and I was punished for crying.

"I'm so sorry," I told him, reaching for his hand. He flinched, holding them out of my reach. "You don't deserve that."

He nodded. "How bad was he?" His voice was so quiet.

"He didn't let me cry. I didn't know what quiet meant until he was gone."

Parker nodded once more before standing up. "Help me... um, help me pick out a new book?"

I smiled, getting up and following him to the shelves.

We walked through the shelves, breathing in the musty scent that old books made.

This library had big open shelves, and when I looked up, the color of the dark and rainy sky against every color you could imagine on the spines of the book complimented each other perfectly.

People were murmuring softly, flipping pages and tapping the keys on their laptops, but Parker and I said nothing.

I pointed at books I thought looked interesting; he looked at them, read the back and slid them back onto the shelve.

"Parker," I whispered. "Why were you on the ground?"

He looked at me, his eyes nervously watching me, and when he answered, his voice was so quiet that I had to lean in to hear.

"I didn't want anyone to find me."

"But I did," I told him.

"You did."

I sat down, leaning against a bookshelf, motioning for him to join me.

"Can I tell you something?" I whispered in his ear.

Parker nodded, his cheeks red.

"When I was a kid, I had an imaginary friend named Edgar, and he never said a single word."

He chuckled, covering his mouth. "Is that supposed to make me feel better?"

"Maybe. Can I pick you up for school tomorrow?"

He nodded, smiling.

"Time to bring you home, I guess."

He was suddenly quiet. I watched as he fiddled with a scrap of paper, worried I had upset him.

"Parker?" He looked up; his brows furrowed. Why did he look so scared? "Are you okay?"

He nodded slowly, standing up.

"We can go if you would like to." He walked away slowly, clutching his book as he went to put it away.

He was making me nervous. Why was he so quiet? Why did he suddenly switch?

"Maybe we shouldn't," I told him when he came back.

"No, you said you were bored, so let's go," Parker said stubbornly, his hands clenching his sleeves.

"Okay," I answered hesitantly. This wasn't okay, this was the least bit okay it could be, because he reminded me of me. I never wanted to go home, not with Stepmonster there, but I couldn't ask him if he had a monster for a family. I knew better than anyone that I couldn't.

I was uneasy the entire way there, wherever *there* was. Parker directed me and I followed. He didn't say anything else and I didn't force him to.

While I drove, I glanced over at him every couple of minutes, like if I wasn't watching, he would disappear. I wouldn't put it past him; he seemed like someone who liked to vanish.

We had talked about so much in such a short amount of time, and yet, I still wanted to hear more, hear the words pour from his lips like the air when he sighs.

I had never felt this way before. I had also never told anyone but Mom that I had issues with being angry, and now Parker knew. Why wasn't I upset? Everything, everyone makes me angry, and sure, I'm able to tie it down for a while, but eventually it comes tearing out, roaring like a dragon coming out of hiding.

And here I was. Sitting next to Parker, a boy whose eyes sometimes sparkle and with cheeks the color of roses. I don't feel the licks of anger curling up my spine

"You can stop here," he told me. "This is my place."

His house was huge and beautiful, painted the same beige that every house on the block was painted. The garden was green and lustrous; hedges lined the walkway and a white picket fence threading the outside of the house. This was not a cheap house. It was a safe neighborhood, something I haven't experienced since I was seven, but safe neighborhoods meant nothing to me when he asked like he was now. Even as I admired the white picket fence, the perfect house, I knew something was wrong.

Parker was gripping the strings of his still damp sweatshirt so tightly I could see his white knuckles. He glanced up at me, his face flickering as he noticed me already watching. He plastered on a calm look, but I could see his hands shaking.

He went to open the door, and I grabbed his shoulder before he was able to leave. I didn't like the way he flinched when I touched him.

"Wait." I tried to think of anything that would keep him here. "I don't feel good about this."

He smiled, but the way his lips pressed together made me even more nervous.

"Eryn, I live here. I'll be fine."

I shook my head, knowing somehow that he wouldn't be fine. I felt frustration build in my chest.

"No, you can stay with me. We can go park somewhere and hang out longer."

"Eryn," he said, shaking his head and placing his hand on my arm. "I'm fine. It's just home."

He opened and got out before I could stop him. He waved, an exhausted smile on his face, and started up the steps. I felt like he was sealing his fate as he hunched his shoulders, his hair drenched once more.

The never-ending sound of rain was slowly but surely ticking me off.

Parker paused at the door, stopping my breath. He waved again before his figure disappeared into his house.

I sat in my car for another 20 minutes. I don't know what I was expecting, maybe to see Parker crash through the door and race to my car, but he didn't. I don't know if I wanted him to or not. I waited, nonetheless.

I drove to Cherry's house, trying to calm myself down before I arrived home, knowing Mom would be concerned, and I didn't feel like explaining myself today.

Seeing Parker for the first time today was amazing, for lack of better words. Everything he did was mysterious, and I wanted to know more. I've always been someone who doesn't care what makes a person them, it's just never been a priority for me. This was not the case for Parker. I felt almost as though he deserved to have someone know him, and damn it, I was going to be that person.

I couldn't think about that now, I had bigger fish to fry, such as the Cherry, a devastating pufferfish that was waiting for her car. That I had.

Just like I thought, she was waiting for me outside her house, arms crossed. I pulled up in front of her, smirking at her as I tossed the keys out the window to her.

"Where have you been? It's been almost four hours since you told me you were going home! I was worried sick!" Cherry said, stalking up to me and poking me in the chest as I struggled to get out of the tiny car.

"I was with Parker. He fell, and I helped him up. We went to the library to hang out, and I guess I just lost track of time," I told her, deciding not to tell her how defeated he had looked when I found him. That was between us.

"The library?" She leaned back on one foot, screwing up her face in a disappointed expression. "That is the worst place to snatch a smooch!"

"We weren't— Cherry! Leave me alone, I'm an adult!" I told her, laughing at her.

"Barely."

"Shut up."

"Cherry!" Marissa yelled from the front door. "Come here, we have to talk about colleges!"

Cherry groaned loudly, giving me the stink eye as she shuffled back to her mom.

I left, jumping into my car—which I had not been able to drive to the café—and pulling out of there as quickly as I could, hoping Marissa wouldn't stop me to talk about college too.

I listened to the car underneath me as I drove, pebbles hitting the tires softly as I drove over speed bumps, and as I thought about everything that had happened today, a deeply uneasy feeling settled over my chest.

Parker really didn't want me to come into his house, or to even get out of the car, so I didn't, but I feel like I should have. I know I should have.

I could hear the yelling the second I got out of my car, loud booming sounds that sent chills of rage down the back of my hands.

I didn't want to walk in. It's my unspoken job to protect my mom from Stepmonster, but every day I wished a little more that he would leave. Honestly, if he stays?

I won't.

chapter four
quiet now

Parker

I shut the front door behind me, trying to stay as quiet as possible. I stopped moving for a moment, stilling my breathing, praying to anyone that could be listening that Father wasn't home.

The table my mom kept by the front door rattled slightly as I held my breath, the small potted plant rocking as I did.

The house was silent. The only thing I heard was the radiator quietly rumbling.

I wasn't used to this. The house being quiet, I mean. Father loves baseball and watches it constantly. He used to watch it with me, and while I've always disliked sports, I used to watch them with him. I tried to earn his pride as I cheered with him when the team we liked hit a home run, and that was the way I knew him, that was the way he knew me.

I've learned to hate it.

I let out a breath, still not hearing any noises, and raced up the stairs, clicking my own door behind me.

My walls were bare. After I came out to my parents, my

mom went on a cleaning rampage, tearing everything down from my walls and stuffing them into the trash, taking everything that meant something to me and shoved it under my bed and in the closet. I remember being distraught that day, not understanding why she would do something like that. She had sat me down, bluntly telling me that if there was one picture of a man on my wall I would be grounded for months.

It was a big enough sign that I was unnatural. Liking a guy was not okay, and I was a monster for doing so. So why did I do that today, when for years I've been shoving those feelings down, doing my best to control that side of me?

I stood in the middle of my room, trying to understand everything that had just happened.

Eryn picked me up. And dropped me off. And brought me to the library when he found me.

I stumbled to the window, hoping to catch another glance.

His car was still here. What is he waiting for? I couldn't see his face through his tinted windows, but I could see the outline of his face, his hands that were tapping the wheel excessively.

I watched his car for another twenty minutes. I wasn't sure if I was waiting for him to leave or to come knocking. I wasn't sure I wanted him to or not.

He left eventually, however. It felt like watching the key to my cell fall just out of reach, and I needed that key more than anything I'd ever needed before.

I spent the rest of the evening doing homework, but even then, he wouldn't leave my mind. I would be doing math equations and accidentally write his name instead of a number. X=2y+Eryn. It happened more than once, and each time, I was infuriated with myself for being so distracted.

I shouldn't be doing this. I'm not the type to scribble names everywhere, so why would I now? What makes him different than every other guy at school?

Maybe it was because he was so eager to know me, to be around me. He wanted to be around me so much that he drove me to the library to help me calm down, despite the fact that he doesn't enjoy reading. Why would he want that? I'm not the most interesting guy out there, I don't do much. Why would he be interested in me?

I couldn't believe he saw me behind the bush. I couldn't believe that he wanted to help me, to get me to a dry place. Nobody had ever done anything like that before. Not even my own parents.

I wasn't called down the dinner that night.

I woke up in a cold sweat, my shirt sticking to me. I couldn't stop my body from violently shaking as I lay in bed, the sheets wrapped around my legs like chains.

I sat up and pressed my hands over my face, wiping my hands against the sheets as I felt sweat drip from my nose.

Another nightmare I couldn't remember. It's happening a lot more lately, my unsettled brain forcing me to wake up terrified but not know what happened.

The clock read 2 AM, the unnaturally green light blinding me as I read. I sighed, knowing I wouldn't be able to fall asleep again. I swung my legs off the bed, wincing at the cold ground under my bare feet and made my way to the bathroom, my hands already twitching.

I locked the door behind me, leaving the lights off. I couldn't bear to see myself right now.

Sitting down in the darkest corner of the room, I tilted my head back, leaning against the wall. The small window let some of the moon's light fall on my legs, making them look fragile.

My chest felt tight, and my hands were clammy as the familiar feeling of anxiety overwhelmed me once more.

How is it possible to know someone for a couple hours and feel like you *know* them? I don't even know his last name; I don't have his phone number!

He might have only been nice to me because that girl Cherry pushed him into it. That would make more sense than him wanting to be nice because he could. I've never understood that, the fact that someone could be nice just because they could. That's insane. It's practically impossible. Everyone has a motive, and when kindness is shown, it's always a motive for something much worse.

Why would he bring me to a library when he hates reading? He could've brought me anywhere else, and he chose the library? I couldn't tell what that said about him, but now, my head was spinning too much for me to care.

When that woman called him over, I knew what she said without hearing her. We were disgusting together, weren't we?

My hand twitched for it, my fingertips shaking as it did.

All I had wanted to do was leave and go somewhere where I would feel safe, and we did leave eventually. But I hadn't wanted to go home either, and I had known that if Father saw him with me, I would be in heaps of trouble. Next time, if there is a next time, I wasn't going to let him get near my house. It's too much of a risk to let him get close.

I wished I could introduce myself differently to him. 'Hey, my name is Parker, I'm cool and casual and single, what's your number?', 'Hi, I'm Parker, a guy who deals with too much of the world's weight on his shoulder, and my bones are crumbling as I struggle to stand, but that's fine, wanna go get food?'

Of course not. Nothing I could've said would make me sound any better than I really am. Still. The thought of him laughing at one of my jokes? Or telling him something about myself that nobody else would ever know?

Here I am though. A pathetic lovesick guy sitting on the floor of a bathroom at 2 AM. What would he think if he saw me now? Would he laugh?

My eyes flitted to the drawer that I tried to keep closed.

No, no, I can't. Not again. I wouldn't be able to stop.

I ran my fingers through my messy hair, hugging my knees close to my chest and forcing myself to look away.

So many sleepless nights. Night after night after damn night. I never win. I don't know if I want to win, but the fight will continue every night until I lose. Some people fight their battles in the daylight, in their sleep, but I fight mine when I am startlingly sober on my own thoughts. When the moon is the only light, I am able to see.

My hand lunged without me telling it to, and the drawer flew open, everything inside crashing into the side with a soft crash.

There it was.

I stared at it, somehow hoping that it would shatter, or someone would bust in, begging me to stop.

But it didn't. The room remained a cell.

All I wanted was control. I can't control my feelings, I can't control my life, and I certainly can't control him.

It glinted in the moonlight when I held it up, and I hated the sight of it more than I hated my own reflection.

I threw it across the room, grabbing handfuls of my hair, trying not to scream. My chest rose and fell quickly, and no matter how many times I swallowed, my throat remained dry.

It hurts, the weight of the heavy world, all these people's lives that belonged to someone else.

My parents' lives that they once had all to themselves. They grew up once, knowing that one day, they might want to have a kid or two, and he would be perfect, the perfect manly guy, the perfect everything. They were wrong. They couldn't have been more wrong.

Their lives are not their own now. I was a part of them, but I was not perfect. I could never be perfect. So, does that make what I'm doing more or less justified?

A soft knocking slowly became louder as I woke up, my head pounding.

Last night I had pulled myself off the bathroom floor and into my bed, exhausted from everything that I had caused. Still, it took me a second to remember where I was.

I got out of bed, pulling on a sweatshirt over the bandages that now covered almost all of both my forearms and slipped on jeans.

When I opened the door, Mom checked down the hall, shoving a brown lunch bag into my hands.

"Your backpack is by the door. Hurry, come on, I can hear your father." Her eyes bounced over me, stopping to glance behind me into my room before her lips pursed in disgust. "Come on, what are you waiting for?"

I jumped at her hasty voice and threw on shoes before racing down the stairs. I knew that my room was clean, I knew that everything was cleaned up and put away neatly, just like Mom wanted it to be. I knew that she was not disgusted by the state of my room, but by the proof that I lived in it that made her purse her lips like that. But she still loves me. Right?

I grabbed the backpack, turning to hopefully hug Mom goodbye. I knew before I saw her that she would not follow me downstairs to say goodbye. She never does anymore.

She was still upstairs, hugging my father. Her eyes were closed. She has always made sure that I knew she loved me, but love isn't the same concept as acceptance.

I bit my lip and backed out of the house, knowing that I wasn't wanted. It was only when I was on the sidewalk when I felt my arm begin to throb.

Perfect.

I stroked the gauze covering the wounds carefully and slid my sleeves back over them, annoyed at the thought of having to be extremely careful with them for a while until they healed.

The neighborhood was quiet, the birds chirping cheerfully in the leaf barren trees as I passed large houses. The sky was still slightly dark, but I welcomed the privacy as I made my way out of the neighborhood and into the main road.

Usually as I walked, thoughts of terrible things filled my unsuspecting head, like dates of tests or you know, life, but today, something was different. I could feel it. Sure, this morning started like pretty much all the other mornings in my entire life, but the universe was looking out for me today.

I could just be extremely sleep deprived, however. Nothing ever goes my way, that's just life, and I suppose I was okay with that.

Life will not stop for me, life will drag me kicking and screaming into the future, even if I desperately want to stay in the past. I should've fixed everything then, because now, life will not stop for anything.

I had been walking to school for almost a half hour when an ugly green car pulled up beside me. I stepped to the side, hoping that whoever was driving would ignore me.

Eryn's face popped out of the window, grinning happily, and I couldn't help but smile back at him.

"Hi! Thought I would drive by and offer you a ride," he said, his voice upbeat.

"Right, um, no, it's okay, it's only a mile or so, I need the exercise anyway," I tried to joke, ruffling my hair nervously.

"You don't. I think you look good now."

"O-oh."

"Uh anyway," he said, his cheeks turning a light shade of pink. "Can I give you a ride?"

"Um," I glanced down the road, trying to see how far I would have to walk. The road stretched on for a couple more miles. I lived far away from the school, more than the mile I had told Eryn I had left. It would be a while longer if I walked.

"Do we even go to the same school?" I asked, stepping back carefully.

"Bersive High School?"

I nodded, surprised we *did* go to the same school.

How have I not seen him already? I imagined Eryn walking by me, bumping into me and apologizing as he walks away. I probably would have nodded, trying to continue staying invisible and would walk away. I wonder if he would stare after me. Would he try to talk to me? Thoughts with the pointed edge of Eryn's smile when he first saw me stuck to my throat like darts, and I swallowed loudly, trying to wash away the dryness away.

Eryn's gaze felt warmer as he leaned over and pushed my door open for me, and I slid in, trying not to let him see how nervous I was, but I was indeed nervous.

He glanced at me with a small smile, biting his lip as he pulled back onto the road. I tried not to laugh at the way he was acting.

"What? What'd I do?" he asked playfully, letting out an amused laugh.

"Nothing you're just acting, uh, cute." I stopped, my face burning.

Eryn's face was frozen in a mask of surprise.

My thoughts picked up in a hurricane of panic. I hoped he wouldn't make this conversation even more awkward by commenting on my stupid words. I should have thought them through, I should've waited to say anything.

It had only been a couple of moments where all words had been abruptly halted, but I felt as if it had been years of silence. I desperately needed something to hold onto, to stop me from slipping into the void of self-hatred.

Then, like he read my thoughts, he looked over at me and winked. "Thanks, you're not so bad yourself." I tried to laugh, but nothing in it was convincing.

His cheeks were still ever so slightly pink, and I'm sure mine were almost purple with embarrassment.

Eryn chatted about anything and everything while I sat in silence, nodding and making sounds of agreement while my mind raced in the opposite direction.

"Parker?" he asked, glancing at me.

"Yeah?"

"Are you okay? I was worried about you last night."

My ears felt hot. "Oh yeah, I'm... I'm fine."

"You don't sound fine."

"I am."

"Are you sure—"

"I said I'm fine!" Even I could hear the shrillness in my voice. "I'm sorry, I just... I'm okay."

"Alright. I didn't mean to pry." His words were soft, and I wished I could've taken my sudden panic back.

I tugged on my sleeve absentmindedly.

The sounds of the road underneath us was the only thing

making noise for a while. It threatened to send me down a path I couldn't afford to go down now.

"So um," Eryn started, biting his lip. "Do you like school?"

I turned to watch him; a bit surprised he still wanted to talk to me. "Do you?" I asked quietly.

He scoffed. "Hell no."

I tried not to smile. "Neither do I."

Eryn didn't respond, but our silence was comfortable now. I didn't feel as though anything needed to be said to keep me grounded. His presence was enough for now, and I was grateful that he had wanted to give me a ride.

I didn't want to leave the car when we stopped at school. Neither of us moved.

It felt very intimate, being so close in proximity with him and not saying a word, the car deafeningly silent now that Eryn had turned it off.

I was about to say goodbye when he said very quietly, "Bye Parker. See you in front after school."

He opened his door and stepped out without another word. I sat in shock for a moment before fumbling for the door handle.

It opened before I was ready, and I spilled out of the car in a whirl of arms and legs. I scrambled to grab my bag and followed him.

"Eryn!"

He turned around with a slightly bemused look on his face.

"Yeah?"

"What'd you mean? By um... in front of the school?"

He was obviously trying not to laugh, his lips pressed together in a line as he watched me jog up to him.

"What?" I asked, crossing my arms in annoyance.

"Nothing." He stopped himself before he said it, but I knew what he wanted to say.

"I'm not cute," I mumbled quietly, hoping he didn't hear.

His stupid grin grew wider.

"What did you mean by meeting you after school?" I

asked again, trying to ignore my fiery face.

"I'm picking you up," Eryn said matter-of-factly.

"What? Why?" My heart skipped a beat.

"Why? Because you live a couple of miles away! I'm not gonna let you walk that far when I have a perfectly good seat open, right next to mine."

"Yeah but—"

"No cuts, no buts, no coconuts."

"What?"

"You've never heard that?"

"No?"

"Hmm." He didn't seem fazed, and he also didn't explain, which made even more confused, a feat that had seemed impossible at the moment. "Anyway, I can walk you to class if you'd like.

"Um…" I wanted to say no, but I hated walking in the halls alone. Eryn looked tall and threatening enough to stop anyone who would've wanted to make fun of me. Even without his protection, I liked his company. "Okay," I said, smiling softly.

He grinned, reminding me of a puppy. "Cool! Lead the way!"

chapter five
call me princy

Eryn

I tried to keep my stride slow enough for Parker, who seemed determined not to tell me to slow down.

"Am I going too fast?" I asked, trying hard not to smile.

"Shut up," he mumbled, his cheeks pink.

Our silence was filled with our chattering classmates. I caught bits and pieces of passing conversations, nudging Parker whenever I heard a particularly strange one.

I couldn't help but notice the satisfied smirk Parker made as a tall guy started to go up to him, but stopped once he saw me, turning around with a disappointed look on his tan face.

"Did you want to talk to him?" I asked him, hoping I didn't scare away his friends.

"No. Let's just keep going," he answered quickly, flashing another soft smile at me.

I couldn't stop the flurry of butterflies from bursting into flight deep in my stomach.

However, I remembered too late why I don't walk anyone to class. I glanced ahead, my stomach dropping at the sight of

Cherry, who was waiting by my locker like she had every day since the fourth grade, looking down at her phone with annoyance carved into her eyebrows.

Crap.

"Hey, why don't we go a different way?" I said, trying to back up. "I think I know a better route."

"But my class is at the end of the hallway," he said, looking confused.

Of course it was.

"I'm pretty sure we have time, let's just hang out a bit longer."

"Why?" He seemed like he wanted to make this difficult for the both of us. He had no idea what he was getting himself into, but I knew that Parker wouldn't let us turn around, not when his class was so close.

"Fine, but I tried to go back. Just prepare yourself," I told him, shaking my head.

"Wait, what? Eryn, what do you mean—"

"*Eryn!*" Cherry's voice practically echoed throughout the hallway. More than a couple people turned to see what had happened, but when there was no fight in front of them, they turned back to their friends.

I winced and grabbed Parker's wrist to pull him forward when he stopped, a bewildered look on his now slightly pale face.

"You're late!" Cherry yelled, stalking towards us angrily. "You know that we meet here every day, and you didn't text me, so what took you—" She stopped, finally noticing a very shocked Parker standing next to me. Her eyes shot to my hand holding Parker's wrist. I dropped his wrist quickly, hoping Parker wouldn't be hurt.

He didn't seem to mind, but I could feel him glancing at me nervously, but Cherry had already seen him, there was no point in running now.

Her expression changed immediately at the sight of him, melting from an annoyed expression to a blissfully polite one.

"Eryn! You didn't tell me about your friend!" She purred,

shooting me a look that very clearly said I would be explaining everything later.

"Yeah, but we—" I tried to say loudly.

"I introduced the two of you, didn't I?" she interrupted, glaring at me.

"Um... yeah," he mumbled, his cheeks turning a deep shade of pink from the sudden attention.

"Cherry, we really have to—"

"Eryn, really, you're being rude." I threw my arms up as she scolded me. "Don't you think he would want to know his boyfriend's best friend?"

"Boy— Wait, Cherry—" I tried to explain, but she wasn't gonna let me talk.

"So what was your name again?" she asked Parker, flashing an intimidatingly sweet smile, but to me, that smile meant that she hadn't even begun.

"Parker, but we're not—"

"Parker! What a great name!" she exclaimed, looking at me like we were buying a puppy.

I tried to get in what we had been trying to tell her, but her voice refused to let a single word through. "Cherry, I swear, if you—"

"Parker, are you new to dating?" He took a step back, looking anxious to leave.

"I um," he glanced over to me. I tried to smile apologetically, although I'm sure it looked more like a grimace. "I have to get to class, so um..."

"Oh sure, go ahead! Can't wait to see you again!" Cherry said, smiling.

He didn't move for a second, watching me carefully. I wanted to go with him, escape from whatever was about to happen, but Cherry grabbed my wrist in a vice, her smile starting to seem more dangerous than kind. Parker seemed to notice now, and his own polite smile dropped suddenly as he dropped his gaze nervously, running his hands through his hair. I felt a pang of guilt in my throat.

He tried to smile again and wave as he backed away, but

he tripped over his own feet, stumbling for a quick moment before looking back nervously and hurrying into his classroom door.

I watched him go, feeling a slow build of familiar frustration build in my chest. How could she do this, how could she even attempt to ruin what I knew I needed so badly?

"Cherry."

"Yes?"

"I told you to stop."

"Yes, you did."

I whirled around to face her and yanked my hand out of her grasp, feeling an angry heat rush to my face as I did so.

"Then why didn't you? You saw that he was uncomfortable, don't lie to me, you knew he was, but you kept going! Why? Do you not have any courtesy for anyone?"

"Eryn, I had to make sure he was good enough for you," Cherry said quietly, crossing her arms curtly.

"That's not your job! You say that every time you see a guy I might like, and you really didn't ask him any questions that would have made sure he was whatever you wanted from him."

She gave me a look when I paused to take a breath. I tried to take another deep breath, knowing this could get much worse if I didn't try to calm down.

"Cherry, I understand what you were trying to do, and I appreciate the effort, but you scare off every guy I'm interested in."

She sighed, blowing pink hair from her face.

"Yeah, but that's not my problem. They just didn't pass."

I glared at her. "I don't want you to scare this one off. He's different. I really like him."

She nodded unhappily.

Cherry is one of the only people who isn't afraid to tell me the truth, but when she does stuff like this, it not only annoys me that she would even try to scare off the guys she pushed me into, but it reminds me of my mom, and as much as I love my mother, I don't like to be reminded of who she once was.

It made everything feel like my fault even when I know it wasn't, it was *his*.

Mom used to be someone I felt safe in telling her my crushes, even when they started to be guys instead of girls. She would go up to them, talking to their parents and convincing them to let me come over and hang out. She was the one who got me my first kiss cause of that.

Her name was Paula, and she was a terrible kisser. She was also the first girlfriend of the two that I had, and both of those relationships turned sour pretty soon after they started. I was still grateful for Mom's help, however.

It's not that I don't feel safe in telling her that stuff anymore, it's just that I suddenly had to be strong for her. She was strong for me every day, taking the brunt of everything while I just sat around, unable to help. I had to pretend that everything was okay, or she would crumble like I knew she wanted to.

The bell rang above us, and the hallway quickly filled with people heading to their first period of the day. Cherry tightened the straps of her backpack, nodding to me as I started backing away from her.

She didn't respond when I said goodbye as I left for my own first class of the day.

School dragged on without another incident, every minute longer than the last. Teachers' and students' voices blended together as the minute hand on the clock ticked by slower than I would've ever thought possible.

I flipped my pencil over and over, so bored I could barely keep my eyes open. The paper in front of me had already been filled out, my messy handwriting scrawled in every blank space.

I couldn't stop thinking about Parker. I was picking him up in mere minutes, and the very idea of him being so close once again was both terrifying and outstanding.

The teacher began yelling at one of the students who had dozed on in class, and I was suddenly grateful that I hadn't fallen asleep yet.

The final bell rang, sending everyone in class scrambling for their things and I shot out of my seat, grabbing my bag and out the door before anyone could stop me.

My heart pounded as I made my way through the crowd. The bodies of students pressed together, and I started to feel the inklings of anger swell in my chest like a balloon, and as some guy slammed his shoulder into mine as he passed, I grabbed the front of his shirt, pulling him close as I grit my teeth.

"Watch where you're going," he said, his eyes narrowed.

I yanked him closer. "Say that one more time," I growled, knowing that if looks could kill, he would be burnt to a crisp.

His eyes widened, and he seemed to change his mind in a split second.

"Sorry man, it was my fault, just let me go," he said, holding up his hands in surrender.

I rolled my eyes, letting go of his shirt with a scoff. He scampered back to his friends, who laughed as he approached.

I had better things to do than mess with some idiot kid. Parker was riding home with me, after all.

Crap. Parker was riding home with me, which meant I had to think of something clever to say to make him laugh, to maybe ask him out or something.

Maybe he won't even show. He could've just decided to walk home without me.

I ducked behind a corner, ignoring the freaked-out glances as I forced myself to take a couple deep breaths.

He'll be here, he will, I told myself, trying my absolute hardest to believe it.

When I peeked out from behind the wall, he stood looking down at his phone, hair covering his eyes across the courtyard. He was actually here.

For a second, I wasn't sure if I was dreaming.

He looked up like he heard my thoughts, his eyes searching the crowd, not spotting me from my very not-clever hiding spot. I could see the brilliant blue of his eyes even from our distance.

I tried to look cool and confident as I turned the corner I had been hiding behind, heading towards him.

His gaze landed on me and, putting his phone in his pocket, waited for mine to reach his with darting eyes.

"Hi," he said softly, scanning the crowd with nervous eyes.

"Hi." I couldn't keep the excitement out of my voice.

His eyes widened for a moment before glancing away again.

"So, shall we?" I asked him, holding my arm out.

He looked around again before nodding, ignoring my outstretched arm. I shrugged, linking our arms carefully and leading him to my car, waving at a group of girls who whispered together, watching us with beady eyes.

Parker tried to pull his arm away, but I held fast, telling him it was just to make sure he didn't lose me as I savored the warmth he emitted.

By the time we reached my car, he was mumbling under his breath, staring at the ground with fabulously pink cheeks. I opened the door for him, grinning as his cheeks turned red now and slid into the car, crossing his arms like a grumpy child.

I tried not to laugh too loudly as I walked to the other side.

The girls continued to watch me, giggling nastily. As they whispered together, I caught certain words like disgusting, and Brett. Shoving down my deeply infused annoyance at their ignorance, I waved once more before clambering into the car and shutting the door.

I didn't say anything for a moment, waiting for a sign or a word of protest from Parker. He was quiet as well; seemingly confused.

"Where are we going?" I asked, wrapping my hands around the steering wheel as I waited for his answer.

"What?"

"Where would you like to go?"

"...Home?"

I sighed. "Boring place to go for a date, but alright."

I started the car and began pulling out when Parker's hand stopped me.

"Wait," he said, looking at me pointedly. "We are *not* going to my house for a date."

"Is that what this is?" I asked innocently.

He blushed furiously. "I mean— that's what— that's what you called it."

"Hmm..." I pretended to think for a moment then shrugged. "Alright. Not your house, so then where to, Princy?"

"Please don't call me that."

"It's your call, Princy." I didn't think it was possible for someone to blush so much. "Where to?" I asked, gentler than time.

"Wherever you want. I don't know a lot of places around here." Parker said, leaning back in his seat and looking out the window.

"So, what I'm hearing is... you'll let me pick?"

Parker looked over at me cautiously. "Um... yeah?"

"And you'll let me order for you?"

"Why would you order for me?"

"I guess I've gotta bring you home..."

"What? Why?"

I shrugged, trying my absolute best not to smile.

"That's ridiculous!"

I looked away, starting to put the car in drive again.

"Alright Fine! You can order for me!" he said loudly, leaning over the console between us.

He stole my breath away, waltzing away with it wrapped around his perfect fingers. His blue eyes blazed, thick brows raised.

Parker noticed my silence and sat back quickly, cheeks pink.

"Okay. Let's go," I said quietly, finally driving out of the parking lot, feeling a little lightheaded.

There was a theme here; the silence that ensues after the car begins moving began once more. I didn't mind too much; the fact that he was here, that he was sitting next to me was joy-inducing enough. I could handle a little silence if it meant he could be beside me.

Even with the outside sounds leaking in through the windows, I was still captivated by the very sound of his breathing. He was breathing next to me, *me* of all people!

I felt the urge to catch his attention again, to make him laugh, to hear everything about him just like I wanted to tell him everything about me.

I wanted to promise him the world.

Man. I've known this guy for a couple days and already, I'm creating worlds for him in my head.

I wonder what his favorite flower is.

"So…" I started, trying to shake off my confining thoughts. "Do you like music?"

He smiled a little. "Yeah."

"What type?"

He sighed, looking up at the roof. "Uh… I like pop, jazz and I guess country."

I turned my head to look at him slowly. "No. Not you," I mumbled.

"What?" he asked, finally looking at me.

"Country? You have got to be kidding me!" I said loudly, hitting the steering wheel.

"Country isn't that bad!" Parker said defiantly.

"Yeah, it is! It's people who have never worked a day in their lives singing about beer and horses! Does that sound like quality entertainment to you?" I questioned, laughing.

He scoffed, shaking his head. I was so very amused by the very aspect of this conversation.

"I can't believe you're one of them." I shook my head in disappointment.

"Eryn, it's really not that big of a deal," he said, shifting in his seat, eyebrows now furrowed.

I grinned. It was fun to get him mad. "Alright, I give. It's perfectly normal to listen to country," I told him. "Especially if your name is Parker."

Parker was quiet for a moment, looking as though he was struggling to find an answer to my teasing. "Do you read?" He asked, a small smile slowly growing on his face.

I rolled my eyes. "Does anyone?"

"Of course! Why do you think there's so many authors in this world?"

"I dunno, I thought people just got bored."

He scoffed. "For someone who has such strong opinions, you really haven't experienced much."

I gasped in mock anger. "Well I'll be a monkey's uncle! The mouse *does* have a tongue."

Parker muttered something unintelligible under his breath, turning to look out the window.

I couldn't help but beam at his turned head. I liked him a lot. I've never liked someone so quickly. Even Cherry was someone I didn't accept into my life until she refused to be ignored. People like Stepmonster would never get there obviously, but Parker is different.

I mean, I've hardly known him for more than three days, and he's barely spoken his mind at all, but when I hear the sass in his voice, I can't help but need to hear what he's passionate about.

I pulled into an empty space in the Sea Soul, a diner that'd been around since before I was born. The people that worked there were practically family, and I knew they would be ecstatic to see me bring someone with me this time rather than come alone and sit in the same booth I've always sat in.

I had been going there for years and years until my dad left Mom and I. We went there to pretend everything was okay. On birthdays, anniversaries, holidays. It worked too; it was like Santa Claus to me. I used to think it was a peace treaty, a way of asking for forgiveness when in reality, it was a forged signature.

The next day, my parents would go back to fighting and I was pushed out of the way.

I guess Mom has never been able to find a good guy. Besides, she doesn't come here anymore. He won't let her.

She doesn't remember it the way I do. She always said it was the calm before a storm, but she's always had this look in her eyes, like she would do anything to go back to that calm.

Now, the neon lights made my hands look blue as I held the door open for Parker. He stepped out carefully, staring down at his feet.

"Nice shoes," I told him.

"Thanks," he answered, one eyebrow raised as he finally looked at, and once again, the sight of his eyes was so brilliant, so different compared to the artificial blue that I lost myself for just a moment.

I closed the door behind him and held my arm out for him. This time, he shook his head slightly.

"I don't think I want to," he said quietly.

I cocked my head, feeling a bit proud as he finally set his true thoughts free, even if it was for just a moment. "It's alright. I'm sorry if I embarrassed you earlier."

He smiled, his eyes twinkling. He didn't say anything, but he didn't need to.

His eyelashes were much longer than I'd thought, the blue light reflecting off them as he blinked. How was I supposed to control my whirling head when even his footsteps gave me butterflies?

We started walking in side-by-side, the world at our backs, the blindingly white sky above us.

"Hold on." I stopped him by the door, wanting to promise him something before he walked in.

"Yeah?" he asked, obviously trying to look casual as his eyes bounced everywhere but to my own eyes.

"I wanna tell you something."

"Go ahead."

All of a sudden, I was struck with a sense of doubt. This guy, this guy who reminded me of something that was too amazing to exist next to me, might be intimidated by me, by my promises to give the world to him.

I shouldn't be this weird. Why am I doing this? Was Cherry right? Was he not enough for me?

I looked at him closer, trying to find something that would convince me that he was enough.

Ah. Almost immediately, I saw the twinkle in his eyes, the uncertainty, but mostly, I watched as his eyes watched me as intently as I was watching him.

They call them mirrors to the soul. If that's true, his soul is as bright as the sun, and I can't wait to burn up in it.

"Can I just say that your eyes are amazing?"

His eyes widened and he looked down as his face turned an even darker shade of red.

"Thanks," he whispered.

"No, I'm serious! I feel like your eyes are the most beautiful eyes I have ever seen, the light hits them in a way that they kinda just glow," I said, making a 'you're blowing my mind' gesture.

"Thank you," he said again, looking up as a small smile rooted in his cheeks. "Really."

I nodded, opening the door for him and bowing gracefully. "Of course, Princy. I would never lie to you."

After a moment of watching me, he looked down, smiling as he entered.

I grinned at the back of his head, absolutely thrilled to show him this place, and to eventually show him the worlds I will have created for him.

Don't get me wrong, this is still weird. I was still taken aback by the very idea that I had actually said something like that to him, but the feeling of immediate stupidity was gone as soon as he smiled, and I had known I said the right thing. Suddenly, it hadn't felt like a massive mistake, it hadn't felt like I was too eager, it felt like I was being honest. And that's all I wanted to be with him.

chapter six
surprisingly okay

As we stepped in, I was hit with the strong scent of fries and cooking burgers, a smell that made my mouth water. I glanced around quickly, not wanting Eryn to think I was judging the pace harshly. It was obvious this was a place very special to him, and I didn't want to break this moment like everything else.

The diner was empty except for an elderly couple sitting at a table that looked like it had been set up specifically for them, but the floors were clean and sparkling, and the kitchen still bustled through the small window that allowed the cooks to see us walk in. I watched as a couple men with graying hair smile as Eryn walked in, and they raised their hands in greeting to him as he did the same.

It was just like the diners you see in movies, black and white floors, red booths, the whole shebang. There was even a picture of Marilyn Monroe in the back corner, hanging over a booth right near the window.

A middle-aged woman waited behind a counter, dressed

in a black uniform with red buttons. The white apron tied over her chest was pristine, a shockingly bright contrast against the black. Her grey streaked black hair was tied up with a thick red scarf,

She had looked up as Eryn opened the door for me, ushering me inside. I felt flushed as I watched her shake her head, a smile growing on her tired-looking face just as it had grown on the chef's faces.

"Hey Martha, how's life?" Eryn asked, sliding his fingers against the smooth counter before resting his hand on Martha's arm affectionately.

"I'm hangin' in there, sweetie, you know I always do. Who's your friend?" She asked, her kind face breaking into a curious smile as she patted his hand.

I blushed, trying to answer, but Eryn grabbed my hand, relieving me of that unearthly pressure of introducing myself and beaming at me, his eyes bright with happiness.

"This is Parker," he told Martha, who glanced at our intertwined hands and looked back to Eryn, her eyes twinkling.

"Well," she started breathily, clapping her hands together. "Pick a booth and I'll get you some coffee."

"Thanks," Eryn said, winking and pulling me gently to the booth in the corner with the picture of Marilyn Monroe above it. I smiled softly. I had known this was the booth he was going to choose.

I tried not to knock anything over as I scooted in while Eryn clumsily sat down as well, sliding in front of me, his ever-resilient smile remaining.

"I can still order for you, right?" Eryn asked, batting his eyes dramatically.

I winced, having forgot about his plea. "Um. I don't know—"

"Please? I won't get anything bad; I swear." He held up his right and crossed an X in the air over his heart.

"Ugh, okay fine, but I don't like mustard, or uh... cilantro."

"Cilantro? Here?"

I shrugged. "You never know. It's just gross. Soapy."

Eryn nodded thoughtfully; his face solemn. He picked up the menu and started reading, but he looked like he was skimming rather than reading.

My mind drifted as he did so. He and Martha seemed close, and judging by the attitude he has towards her, it seemed like she was his mom or something. She was a lot shorter than him however, and he was built like a lacrosse player, and they really didn't look related to each other. The only thing that was kinda similar between them was the twinkle in their eyes and their broad shoulders.

"Um." I tried to clear my throat before speaking, my mouth suddenly dry at the thought of being wrong and embarrassing myself in front of him. "Is she your mom or something?"

Eryn looked up at me, his face contorted into a confused expression. "What?"

I coughed again. "Um, is she— uh, she—" I took a deep breath, doing my best to ignore Eryn's encouraging smile. "Is she related to you?" I finished quietly.

"Nah, but I've known her for a really long time, since I was about four, I think."

I nodded, wringing my hands nervously. This was a mistake. I shouldn't have said yes to this; I knew I was going to be a mess. He's going to find out how disappointing I really was, and I didn't know if I could deal with that.

Did I really care though? I looked up at Eryn, who had gone back to the menu, his eyebrows furrowed as if choosing what I was going to eat was a life or death situation.

Maybe not.

But he was so eager, no one has *ever* been eager to see me. I don't know how to feel about that. Eagerness was a trick, a way to force someone to think everything is okay, right? I've never known anything different. Even my own parents, who had sworn they loved me, were never eager to spend time with me. If anything, they avoided it.

I think Father had been looking for a reason to hate me though, so when I told him I was gay, he took the chance. It's not like he's always pretended I never existed, there was a time where he would heckle me as I walked in through the front door, calling out insults when I scrambled up the stairs, rolling his eyes when he saw me eating breakfast in the mornings. That wasn't much better, but at least he acknowledged my existence.

Everything changed that one night though. He was drunk on whiskey and I came home late. He had been waiting for me to get home, but I knew the second I walked in that he was not worried about my safety, but worried that I had told someone, that I had spilled his deep shame of his own son.

I remember it so clearly and foggily at the same time. I don't remember what he had been screaming, but I remember how loud he was, I remember the feeling of his tight grip on my wrist as he drunkenly pulled me forward, I remember the bottle shattering against the doorframe after he had followed me upstairs and the glass and whiskey that showered me before I slammed the door and locked it. I remember the nicks the glass had left on my neck, and the feeling of pure loneliness as I pulled on sweatshirts to cover the cuts.

After that night, Mom had started to avoid me as well, to protect me she said, but lately, I think she just doesn't want to lose her husband over me. I guess she's chosen her side, and that loneliness haunts me every single damn day.

"Parker?" I looked up, snapping out of the whirlpool I was creating. "Do you want a milkshake?" Eryn asked, the menu now folded in front of his still hands.

"Oh. Yeah, chocolate, if that's okay," I responded, slightly surprised to see Martha in front of the table, a purple pen and small notebook in her hands.

"Alright honey, I'll bring that out in a minute," she said, giving me a warm smile and shooting Eryn a knowing glance.

He rolled his eyes playfully as she grabbed our menus and shuffled away.

"Anyway," Eryn started, folding his hands under his chin and leaning towards me, eyes bright. "What'd you think of Cherry?"

I laughed suddenly, startling myself. "She was... interesting."

He shook his head, but a small smile remained on his face. "Yeah, that's one way to describe her. I'm sorry if she scared you, she means the best, she really does, but she's just been waiting for me to 'hook a man.'" I couldn't help but grin at his air quotes.

"She was pretty intense, especially when she asked if we were, uh," I pointed at myself then at him, trying to stop this conversation from happening.

"If we were what?" He asked, his smile turning slightly arrogant.

"You know... er," I waved my hand in a circle, my face so hot I was sure Eryn could feel the heat coming off it.

"I really don't know, care to explain?" he asked, raising his stupid eyebrows.

"Not particularly," I mumbled, looking away from his twinkling eyes.

"It's not very nice to keep someone in the dark."

"When she asked if we were uh, dating."

"I'm not sure that's what she said exactly."

I huffed loudly. "Eryn, you know exactly what she said."

"Mmmm, I don't think I do; you should tell me just in case."

"When she asked if we were boyfriends," I said quickly, not wanting to draw this awful conversation out longer.

He grinned, making an exaggerated 'Aha!' face. "I do remember that. Why did that scare you?" he asked, leaning back and crossing his arms, a self-satisfied smile on his face. "I mean, you of all people, the mighty mouse."

I opened my mouth to speak but all that came out was a squeak.

Immediately, my face went ablaze, and all I wanted to go home to someone who didn't hate me.

"Hey, don't be embarrassed, it happens to the best of us," he said, sliding his hand over mine on the table.

My eyes shot to our hands, my heart racing. I really hoped he didn't notice how clammy mine was.

"When I was in middle school, my voice cracked all the time. It was usually fine, nobody would really comment on them, but there was this one girl who constantly mocked me for it," Eryn told me, either not noticing my eyes continuing to flick back to our hands and back to his face or choosing to ignore it. "I didn't do anything about it, and eventually she stopped, but she was furious that I wouldn't give her the attention she wanted."

I was quiet, grateful for the distraction. "Why didn't you report it?"

"Because it was Cherry."

Shock rippled through my body as I realized what he had said. "What? Cherry? How did you guys become such good friends when she bullied you?"

He sighed, running his hands through his hair. "I guess she'd just been mean because her parents spoiled her, and she didn't know the right way to act, as ridiculous as it sounds. So, when she made fun of me, I didn't act the way she wanted me to. One time, she came up to me and yelled for a solid minute, and then I punched her." He smiled, a nostalgic look glazing his eyes over. "We hung out a lot more after that."

"And that made you guys friends?" I asked, furrowing my eyebrows.

"Yeah."

It was my turn to sit back and cross my arms.

If Cherry had bullied me, I would've avoided her as much as possible. I would've tried to get away. I was used to it; I could've gotten away.

Bullying was that sort of thing where teachers tell you that it's important to look out for one another and stand up for a stranger when they are in trouble, but that doesn't really happen a lot anymore. When it does, everyone thinks it a joke, and in the beginning, I did too, but the joke went too far. I was left standing in the dust as everyone passed by, laughing as dirt was caught in my open wounds. Why wouldn't they care? So many of them swore up and down that they would truly stop a bully, but their words meant nothing in the long run.

I'm still here though. And I'm here with Eryn, who seemed to have a soft spot for the misunderstood. Is that all I am? A poor misunderstood soul?

"Here ya are kids," Martha said, carrying a large plastic tray with two burgers and two milkshakes on top. "Two fried chicken burgers without mustard—" Eryn winked at me and I blushed again. "And two chocolate shakes with whipped cream."

"Martha, you are a godsend," Eryn said, his eyes fixed on all the food in front of us.

"Thank you," I said quietly, rubbing the heels of my hands together.

"You're very welcome," she replied, ruffling Eryn's hair before making her way to the other customers that had just walked in.

I watched as Eryn practically drooled over the food, but he waited, watching me expectantly. I made a face at him, feeling my heart skip a beat when he grinned widely.

"What?" I asked, feeling nervous as he watched as I picked up the burger.

"Take a bite," he said, leaning forward slightly.

"Why're you watching me like that?"

"I wanna see your reaction."

I stuck my tongue out at him, feeling slightly overwhelmed at his sudden direct attention. The second I took a bite of the God-given burger I sat back in bliss, chewing slowly.

"Yeah, it's the best burger in Seattle," Eryn said, starting on his own burger.

I almost wanted to cry; I can't believe that food could taste this good.

"Parker?"

"Hmm?"

"You have something on your face."

My face was aflame as I reached for a napkin. "Gone?" I asked after wiping my face.

He shook his head.

"Here." He reached out, brushing the corner of my lips with his calloused thumb. "All gone."

I was frozen, speechless. Even my thoughts refused to gather together.

What is this? That was a movie move, the move that all of the male interests pull to make the female interest swoon. Where am I? What is happening? I cannot be the person he's interested in; he must think I'm someone different than I actually am.

I reached for my shake, my hands shaking.

"You blush a lot," he said, his deep brown eyes studying me intently.

Well, duh. I could feel my face already growing warmer at his comment.

It made me a target for bullying, a bright red sign on my pale face. It was mostly Father though. He wanted me to do 'manly things', like help him fix the car, or play baseball with him or something. But I didn't like doing that stuff. I still don't. I blushed when I messed up, and I always messed up. He'd tell me to man up, even when I had been trying my best. Surprise surprise, I wasn't good enough for him.

Now that I thought about it, I wonder if I was ever good enough for Mom too? She never talked to me like Father did. He hurled the words he spoke, not caring whether or not they bruise your skin, but Mom was always careful, picking her words carefully, making sure everything sounded right before they left her lips.

She once caught me wrapping my biceps up after a particularly bad night. I won't ever forget the look on her face. I had been expecting her to be upset, sobbing or forbidding me from ever doing it again, and to be honest, I had hoped she would. But she didn't. She asked what I was doing, and when I didn't answer, she closed the door and never talked about it again, like it was something she didn't care enough to remember. Like it wasn't important enough.

She never really tried to make it seem like she was always there for me. Instead, she strived to prove Father that she was there for him, and she cared for me like a mother would to her child's fish: she fed me and kept me alive, but she didn't show me the same love as she did to Father.

"Do I?" I mumbled, bushing hair out of my face.

"Yeah. Happens when I compliment you," he said, his smile slowly growing.

I grunted in response, picking at my nails.

"Maybe I should do it more. It's cute."

"Ha, I uh," I laughed awkwardly, trying to make it seem like I didn't care when I obviously did care a lot. "Maybe you shouldn't."

"Why not? I wouldn't be lying."

"Sure."

"I'm not kidding!"

I laughed, feeling deeply uncomfortable at his kind words. "I just blush a lot. I can't stop it."

"I'm kinda glad. I like it, I'd be missing a lot if I couldn't see it."

How am I supposed to react to that?

I felt a prick of annoyance as my heart sped up again, excited by his words. My heart and my head felt like two different people, like my heart wanted to know him better than anyone ever would but my head knew that this was going to be a very terrible idea. I feel more inclined to trust my head.

I focused on my shake, realizing both of our burgers were gone. "Oh."

He chuckled. "Sorry, I didn't mean to make it awkward."

"You didn't," I answered, lying through my teeth. Of course he did. How do I change this conversation? "I just uh... yeah."

He sighed, nodding. "Yeah. I get that."

I hadn't even said anything; how could he know exactly

what I meant?

"So. Um, do you—"

"You guys ready for the check?"

Oh thank God.

We were both so hungry from everything the day had piled on top of our shoulders that we had unknowingly scarfed down our food like we hadn't eaten in weeks.

I felt slightly disappointed that we had finished so quickly. I shook my head quickly, trying to shake off that feeling. Even so, when I looked over at Eryn, his content look assured me that this would not be the last time we went out together, and the butterflies in my stomach leaped into the air once more.

"Yep," Eryn said, reaching for his wallet. "I got it."

"Hold on, I can pay for my own," I told him, searching for money I knew I didn't have.

"Don't worry about it, I just got paid." I knew that was a lie, he would've had to work around this time if he did, and that made me feel worse, that he was lying to make me feel better.

"Come on, I can do it, just give me a second to find—"

"Parker." I looked up, my fingers still digging in my pockets. "I got it this time. You get it next time."

I nodded silently, embarrassed as I watched Eryn hand Martha a bill.

She smiled and said something to him, but I couldn't hear them over my pounding heartbeat.

Martha waved at me, a comforting look on her face before leaving.

"Hey." My ears caught his voice clear as day over my everything and I looked up to see him reaching for me. I flinched when he grabbed my wrist despite seeing him before I felt his grasp.

"Hey, Parker, it's fine. I promise I'll go wherever you wanna go next time. I'll be sure to order a steak," he said, winking.

"Next time?" I asked, my voice cracking.

His eyes suddenly became guarded. "Not if you don't want to," he said, his words suddenly stiff.

"No uh... oh wonderful, sorry, you misunderstood," I stumbled over my words as we both made our way out of the diner. "I think I could be cool, you know, to go out again."

Eryn ran his hand through his hair, letting out a nervous laugh.

"Yeah, it would be. Sorry for being rude, I just uh...yeah."

He sounded just as nervous as I felt.

"We should play a game," I said, trying to make things less awkward.

"Sure," Eryn shoved his hands into his pockets as we began walking down the sidewalk. "What's the game?"

"I ask you a question, you answer and vice-versa."

He was quiet for a second. "That's not a game."

"It's close enough to a game."

Eryn was again silent before bursting into laughter.

My face burned as he clutched his stomach, but even then, his laughs felt so amazing, like something I had craved for all my life without knowing I craved them.

"Stop laughing! It wasn't funny!"

He sucked in a breath and tightly pressed his lips together. I watched him cautiously, positive he would break any moment.

"So is that a no or...?"

Eryn practically burst at the seams, tears suddenly streaming from his eyes.

I mentally punched myself for bringing up such a stupid idea. I should've known, but I've never had a boyfriend before—I mean a date I guess—how would I know that going out and making up games would be such a terrible idea?

I glanced over at him, feeling somewhat proud of causing him to throw his head back like that, to clutch his stomach and squeeze his eyes shut as laughs bubbled out of him like a boiling pot.

"Yeah," Eryn said, wiping tears off his pink cheeks. "We can play that." He covered his mouth as another round of giggles forced their way out of his chest.

"Then stop laughing!"

"Alright, you stop yelling and let's start."

I thought for a moment before saying, "Favorite color?"

"What?"

I blinked at him, feeling confused.

"I mean, I thought we were gonna get deep or something," Eryn said, rubbing his stomach.

"Why would we? It's the first date, after all."

He shrugged. "Black."

"No, an actual color."

He gave me the side-eye before saying, "Purple."

I nodded, feeling triumphant.

"I gotta sit down, my abs hurt," he said, gesturing towards a nearby bench. I looked up, surprised to see a park surrounding us. Evergreens towered over us, dripping from the last misting rainfall. I could hear kids screaming with delight from a swing set somewhere, hidden in the trees.

We both sat down, wincing at the sodden seat.

"What's your favorite color?" he asked.

"Light blue, I think."

"That's a good one."

I chuckled, leaning back and taking a deep breath.

Eryn slid his arms on the back of the bench, a small smile on his face.

I could feel the heat from his arm near my neck, and I tried not to move, shivering from the feeling of warmth.

"What's your worst fear?" I asked, hoping I didn't overstep but feeling like I needed to know at least one thing that means something to him.

He was quiet for a moment, staring off into the trees, deep in thought. This was too much. I just said I wasn't going to get deep, but here I am, asking him a deep question like this.

"Hand lotion." He said, nodding like he was agreeing with himself.

"You're kidding me," I said, turning to face him on the

bench. "Hand lotion? Why in the world would you be afraid of that?"

"I don't like the silky feeling after I put it on," he said, shrugging. "It's too soft."

"What— it's supposed to make your hands soft! That's why it was made!"

"Why does it always have to smell like cotton candy though?" he asked, shuddering like we were talking about spiders. "Can't it just not smell?"

"Eryn. First of all," I started, holding up one finger. "Not all hand lotion smells, and second, how is that your deepest fear? You're not afraid of the unknown or something?" He looked up, his eyebrow twitching slightly before looking back at me, shaking his head.

"Nope. Hand lotion is terrifying."

Lies. I do not believe him, but now is not the time for pushing him into answering me.

"Tell me about her," I said, nudging his arm. "Your mom."

He sighed, running his fingers through his hair. "Like what?"

"Who is she? What kind of person does she want to be? You know, like normal questions someone would ask another person?"

"Uh..." Eryn looked over at me before tugging the collar of his jacket. "She's good. Funny. She's kind of like you, actually. I mean, she is now, but she used to be larger than life, you know? Like Cherry."

I nodded, hoping he would continue speaking in the deep nostalgic sounding voice that I didn't know he had.

"She used to leave notes all around the house, to herself, to me, the neighbors, anyone and everyone. She always signed her name at the bottom with 'I enjoy your existence,' like she had something to prove to everyone." He paused, taking a moment to look around us.

The sky was almost a blinding white, covered in a thick layer of clouds that almost looked like cotton balls, and the deep green trees reached for them with outstretched branches.

"What kind of person was she was your next question, right? She was that kind of mom who kissed your forehead every night before bed, you know?" Eryn's eyes lit up. "One time, when I was younger, I'd been playing in the mud outside, so naturally, as little kids so wrongly believe, it was perfectly acceptable to come in the house covered head to toe in mud." He shook his head, smiling as he traveled back in time to that moment. "I can't tell you how upset she was. There was mud everywhere! All over the walls and couch and stuff. She had to chase me down to give me a bath, and she literally tackled me to get me to stop running around."

I laughed, deeply amused at the thought of Eryn as a little kid.

"Yeah. She was great. She still is, she's just uh... different now," he said, shaking his head. His eyes suddenly snapped back to mine, and he bumped his shoulder against mine. "What about yours?"

"Mine?" I asked, feeling my face heat up.

"Yeah. Who's your mom?"

"She's uh... normal. She says she loves me and stuff, but uh, yeah. I'm not really close to my parents."

"How come?"

I looked over at him, wary of the topic. Eryn's eyes darted over the landscape in front of us. His lack of eye contact was enough to make me comfortable enough to continue speaking.

"They're out a lot. I stay in my room most of the time, and they don't bother to say hi or goodnight or whatever. I guess they just kinda don't care." I responded, tugging my sleeves over my fingertips.

"I'm sure they do," he said, finally locking eyes with me.

"I don't think... so..." I let the sentence trail off as we continued to watch each other, the small space on the bench between us feeling smaller with every second that passed.

He really truly thought they did. Doesn't he know that life doesn't work like that? People don't care unless they have to.

They just don't. I would know that better than anyone.

I broke the eye contact first, looking down to fluff my hair, resting my elbows on my knees as I leaned forward to avoid the comforting heat his arm produced near my neck.

He breathed out slowly when I did, and Eryn's scent of leather and soap made me feel surprisingly okay despite my currently flaming face.

He sighed heavily again, crossing his legs as he leaned his head back and closed his eyes. His face looked peaceful, content, like my presence was all he needed.

He was different than I thought he was. He was strange to me, calling me out on my blushing yet brushing it off when it overwhelmed me. Usually, my mom would've ushered me out when Father began pointing that stuff out.

Eryn seemed to actually care. Why was that so foreign? To know that at least someone likes me? As if reading my thoughts, Eryn opened his eyes and smiled warmly at me before reaching for my hand. His fingers brushed the edge of the bandages that covered my shame, and I flinched, pulling away from him quickly.

In an instant, Eryn was awake, leaning forward, his smile suddenly evaporating. "What was that?" he asked, his eyebrows furrowed. "Did you hurt yourself or something?"

I shook my head, pulling my sleeve down further, startled by his intense gaze.

Eryn's eyes narrowed. "Did someone hurt you?"

Again, I shook my head, unable to find the words to tell him I did this to myself.

"You would tell me if someone did, right? Promise me you would." I could see the worry in his eyes so clearly it was like looking through water, and it surprised me.

I took a deep breath before saying, "Eryn, I'm okay, you just... shocked me."

"No, you hardcore flinched, that couldn't have been a shock."

"It was, it just scared me."

His eyes searched mine, the concern blocking me from

seeing *him*.

"Promise me."

"I will. I promise."

He visibly relaxed, his shoulders going slightly limp and nodded.

"Can I hold your hand? Is that okay?" he asked cautiously. He sounded so nervous. Who would be so scared of me? I am the least scary person on the planet. I'm too short, too weak, too much for anyone to handle in the worst way. Why would he, a tall and strong-looking guy, fear someone so pathetic?

I smiled despite my thoughts, holding out my hand carefully.

He took it, grinning. His palm was warm and dry while mine was covered in a sudden slick layer of sweat.

I took my hand out of his grasp and wiped it against my jeans before grabbing his again.

"Sorry."

"You should be. Gross, you sweat? I only produce fresh water with a hint of lemon," he said, winking at me.

"You're so stupid," I said, rolling my eyes.

Hand holding was less romantic than I'd once thought. It's sweaty, and my palm slides against his, but I loved it more than anything. I loved that he wanted to hold *my* hand, that I didn't have to ask him to. It was already on his mind.

The sun went down quicker than I expected, but each moment that we were there felt like the best lifetime I could dream of, and as we walked back, he still held my hand.

His favorite animal was a duck, by the way.

He drove me home, and like most of our drives together, we were quiet. He kept glancing over and grinning like I was his favorite gift on Christmas that he just couldn't wait to see. Each time he did, my heart floated a bit higher, and I swear it brushed the clouds.

After he had started driving, I suddenly got a pang of... something. Panic. The closer we got to my house, the more nervous I got, the faster my heart pounded. Father must have known I wasn't home yet, and even if he didn't, he would know when I walked in.

Eryn couldn't be there when he found out.

"Um, you can drop me off here," I told him, pointing to a space nearly a block away from my house. "I live really close."

"Why don't I just drive you all the way up like last time?" he asked, continuing to drive closer and closer to my—

"No, drop me off here, did you not hear me the first time?" I asked loudly, digging my fingernails into my palms painfully.

Eryn didn't say anything, but he pressed his lips into a hard line as he stared straight ahead. The car pulled up to the curb and I waited for the harsh feeling of the stubborn brakes, but it never came.

My face was hot, and I couldn't breathe right, my chest too tight and my mouth too dry. Everything felt like too much, too much air, too much silence, too much of this suffocating silence that I couldn't stop; my ears rang as the sound of nothing continued.

"Please unlock the door," I said quietly, my heart racing, half speaking to him, half trying to stop the ringing.

Eryn turned to me, studying my face intently. I felt a pulse of self-hatred flow shock my body as his eyes flicked over my face intently. I've messed up twice now, letting him see how truly messed up I was. I have to get better at this.

"You promise?"

"What?"

"Why don't you want me near your house, Parker?" The sound of my name from his lips made me feel dizzy, and this time, I didn't know if that was a good thing.

"My dad… he's sick."

"Sick?"

"Yeah, I just don't want you to catch anything. So drop me off here." I hoped Father wasn't home to see my red face when I walked in.

"Okay…" Eryn said, his voice practically dripping with suspicion. I knew he didn't believe me, but honestly, in the moment, I couldn't care less if he believed me or not.

I tried the door again. It remained locked, a terrifying reminder that I was not in control.

"Please let me out, Eryn."

He didn't move. My heart dropped at the thought of him not letting me leave, but he turned and flipped a switch. Funny, my heart dropped farther when he did.

I opened the door and stepped out quickly, grabbing my bag and slinging it over my shoulder.

"Thanks," I whispered.

He nodded. "Stay safe."

The setting sun seemed to drop out of the sky as he drove away, and I shivered when the light emitted from his car disappeared into the now dim light.

I tugged my sleeve down as I walked the block to my home, feeling my heart pound louder with every step. My mouth tasted metallic.

When I reached the steps, I could hear a baseball game through the door, and I knew I had been gone for too long.

I couldn't move. The sound of the game squeezed my brain until I felt my head get lighter, like I was watching my body from afar. How strange that sensation was. If I shook my head, I was sure that my mind and thoughts would snap back to my body, but I didn't want to. I didn't want to keep them here. They should leave this.

My hand shaking, I opened the door and my father's game was too loud all too soon.

chapter seven
boom, there it is

Eryn

He was lying. He was totally lying, but I didn't want to scare him away, so I let him get out of my car, just like last time. I left before I grabbed his hand and pulled him back in, despite wanting to do just that so badly.

I had my own battles to face tonight.

It was Friday, which meant that Stepmonster was out drinking with his lowlife friends.

Mom was probably still home alone—she never hung out with Marissa or her friends since she married Stepmonster, but I remember when she did. They would sit and drink wine with ice cubes, clinking them every time one of them said something profound or relatable. Cherry and I would watch with wide eyes, doing the same thing but with juice boxes. Mom and Marissa were ecstatic to see us do it together. But that was a long time ago.

I pulled up to my own home, surprised that Parker lived closer than to me than I'd thought. That was good, that was really good. I could pick him up at his front door if I wanted to.

I knew he wouldn't want me to do anything like that though, so I wouldn't, but I could. That's what matters.

Stepmonster's car was gone (no surprise there), but I heard soft music coming from the house, which *was* new.

I smiled before grabbing my bag, feeling a bit nostalgic as I stomped up the porch steps.

The door was locked, so I rapped my knuckles against the wood quickly, twice fast and one slow. The music suddenly shut off, and the door slowly creaked open, revealing a crack of my mom's pale face.

"Hey, baby," Mom said, smiling softly.

"Hi, Mom," I replied, hugging her.

She was thin and too small. It made my chest ache for her. She doesn't deserve to live like this, to be treated this way.

"I made dinner, so get in here and wash your hands," she said quietly, turning the classical music up once more.

She's always loved classical music. She would listen to it with Marissa when they were still friends. They would dance around the house, never allowing Cherry or me to join until they figured out that we were friends. After the day they brought us home from the office after I punched Cherry, they turned on the music and made us waltz with them. It was one of those days I will never forget.

When I was younger, Mom would tell me to close my eyes and imagine the violins sprouting wings, and I would dream of them at night.

She doesn't really say much of that anymore.

Mom gestured to the pot of gumbo on the stove as I dried my hands. I grinned, pulling two bowls from the drawers. Despite the meal I had eaten with Parker only a couple of hours ago, I was starving. The smell of Mom's food will always make me hungry.

"Did you eat, Mom?" I asked, already scooping the deliciously spicy gumbo into a bowl for her.

"No, baby, but I'm not hungry, I don't want any." She kept her eyes closed and she swayed to the music, arms wrapped around herself.

"Too bad. If there's not enough, I'll share mine with you," I told her, handing her the food and grabbing spoons, jerking my head towards the table.

We talked quietly while we ate, like someone was sleeping in the other room. I guess there could have been, what with the many drunk friends Stepmonster seems to have.

"So, Mom," I started, shoveling food into my mouth. "When was the last time you went on a vacation?"

She froze for a moment before continuing to chew slowly. "Vacation?"

"Yeah. Like camping or going to the beach or something."

She shook her head, glancing at the door then to the clock on the wall.

"We should go this weekend!" I said, forcing excitement into my voice.

"No, your—" She stopped, seeming as sick to her stomach as I was to mine. "Greg needs us home."

"Screw Greg. He's never done anything good for us anyway," I said, standing up and putting our empty dishes in the sink.

"Please don't say that," Mom said, straightening her dress as she began to clean up.

"Mom, you hate wearing dresses!" I yelled, feeling guilty when she flinched. "You used to say the day you wore a dress was the day you went to see Jesus."

She was so small, so nervous, but I couldn't stop myself. I've done too much stopping today, I can't stop anything anymore.

"Stop letting him control you! You can't be controlled! You used to be so happy and now you can't even go outside without his permission!"

"He was a good man, baby. He needs us."

"He's not a good guy anymore! And damn right he needs us! But we don't need him. He doesn't deserve you." I grabbed her hands and squeezed them tight.

"Please don't—" Click.

We both heard it. The lock.

I didn't realize how much time had passed while I was gone. I don't think either of us did.

Mom started pushing me to my room, shushing me as I pushed against her.

"Stop, Mom. Stop," I whispered, trying not to let him know where we were.

His slurred voice was getting louder yelling something unintelligible, and the laughter that followed made my blood boil, but all I heard was my Mom's shaking voice as she sang the song that she used to make my nightmares disappear. It was so familiar. Was this what this was to her? A nightmare? Damn nightmares, they're not supposed to happen during the day.

She smiled and kissed my cheek before pushing me into my room and locking the door from the outside, the familiar click shocking me from my thoughts, my muscles tensing instinctually.

An addition Stepmonster had added.

I blinked, suddenly alone in my room, my empty room.

I slammed my fists against my door, my fists pounding the same dents I always pounded, pleading for my mom, begging for her to come back so we could hide together.

I quieted when I heard the loud rounds of laughter strike the air like a punch, and Mom's voice followed, wavering like a ripple in a pond, but I still couldn't hear anything they were saying.

They stopped suddenly, and after a moment, I heard a loud smash of glass breaking.

I couldn't hear the words yelled, but I was shaking with anger as I slid down the door and wrapped my arms over my head while I listened to Stepmonster yell and Mom hum loudly, trying to drown out his voice for me.

My back slammed against the ground as my door suddenly

opened, and I woke up gasping for breath.

"Eryn, baby, it's time for school." Mom's voice was shaking. "Eryn?"

"Mom, are you okay?" I asked, reaching for her as I scrambled up.

She ducked her head as she mumbled it was time to eat, hurrying away.

He hit her. I know he did, he does this every time he gets drunk. Nearly every morning after he does, she gets me up for school and gives me lunch. It's always Saturday, and she always makes me a brown lunch bag filled with whatever leftovers she could find, and I hated the color of those bags, they were disgusting. It made my skin crawl.

I quickly changed before heading into the kitchen, preparing myself for something bad.

I could hear Mom's spatula scrape the bottom of a pan as she cooked. She was silent otherwise, and while that was normal, it still made my face warm with anger.

"Mom, what's going—" I stopped.

Stepmonster sat at the table, looking hungover and annoyed, a plate of scrambled eggs in front of him.

"If it isn't the laziest person in the house," he said, wrinkling his sweaty nose. "Second laziest." He shot Mom a stone-cold glare. She looked to the side as she served him more food, her hair covering her face.

"Don't talk to her like that," I mumbled through my teeth.

He ignored me, complaining about something Mom had done, but she shot me a look, and finally I saw.

"What happened to your face?" I asked, reaching out for her once more, but again, she backed away.

Her skin was bright red under her brow and cheekbone, a bit of purple already leaking through the otherwise pristine skin and most of the left side of her face was swollen.

"Her own fault," Stepmonster said from behind me. "Fell and hit the stove."

I turned to face him, gritting my teeth.

He stood up and shoved his now-empty plate into my

stomach.

"Clean it up," he whispered harshly.

His knuckles were cracked and had scabs decorating them like tacky rings. His hands were swollen, bloated from the beer he loved to chug, and the very sight of his hands made me want to hurt him.

I lifted my head to look straight into his eyes, his nose inches from mine.

"One day, you'll pay for every bruise on her face," I spat, my voice poisonous.

He chuckled, glaring at Mom again before looking back at me with an evil grin. "Yeah? And who's gonna stop me? You?" He laughed loudly again, opening his mouth wide and letting eggs drop down his chin.

I ground my teeth together. "Yeah. Someone like you will be easy to take down."

Stepmonster's smug smile dropped like the sweat from his forehead.

He stepped even closer, but I wasn't going to back down. Not this time.

"You'd better watch what you're saying, boy, or there'll be more than bruises on her."

I glanced at Mom. She was shaking, but the stern look she gave me clearly said to back off, and that was stronger than her fear.

I did what she wanted, grabbing the lunch Mom had packed and stormed past Stepmonster.

A flash of guilt stopped me, and I ducked to hug her.

"I love you, baby," she whispered.

"I love you too."

I left the house as quick as I could, getting as far as the main road before realizing I still held Stepmonster's plate in my white-tipped fingers.

I didn't think for once, I pulled over and got out, smashing the dirt plate against the ground with all my might, wanting to scream.

I knocked on the door, still shaking with rage.

I heard yelling come from inside, and loud footsteps pounded closer, but this time, the very noise set me off more, rage filling my entire body.

Cherry opened the door, her short hair twisted into a bun. She had a bright red lipstick mark under her right eye.

"Hey," she said, glancing down to my hands where the lunch bag was starting to rip in my grasp. "Come on in."

I followed her inside where Marissa took the bag from me and kissed my cheek. She smoothed my hair affectionately, and I leaned into her touch, wishing so desperately that her hands were Mom's.

Cherry led me upstairs to her room, where clothes and makeup covered every inch of her usually clean floor.

I threw myself onto her bed ruining the look of the made bed, covering my eyes.

How the hell was I going to survive this? Was Mom going to survive this? How am I going to get her out of this mess? I honestly have no idea if it's too late or not, but it feels like this is no longer a battle. It's a war.

I wish she could get me out first, as selfish as that sounds. I wish I wasn't the one who had to be this way, to be angry. I want her to stand up for herself. I want her to stand up for me, but she couldn't do that. She just couldn't.

I don't know how long I stayed there, listening to Cherry open and close makeup, mumbling to herself quietly.

The bed dipped beside me when she finally sat down, resting her hand on my shoulder.

"I'm sorry."

I nodded, eyes still closed. Sorry means nothing in the long run. It might mean something to those who need to hear it, but I've heard it so many times that it means nothing anymore.

After another short silence, she said, "You're coming to work with me."

"I don't want to work today."

"I'm not asking you to work, I'm telling you that you

should come and hang out."

I didn't say anything. I was too angry to do that today; everything felt like too much for me to bear. Everything was able to annoy me, everything was able to make me think of Mom, who was trying to cling to anything that kept her alive.

Cherry nudged my knee playfully, snapping me out of my spiral. "Come on, I'll give you a free coffee."

My lips twitched. "Alright, fine."

"First, help me find a jacket."

"You know I only wear this leather one," I said, tugging on the collar. "How am I supposed to decide for you?"

"We'll match!"

"Ugh, your car smells so old," I said as we stuffed ourselves into Cherry's tiny car.

"You say that every time you get in, and like I've said every time, that's because it *is* old. And by the way, thanks for bringing it back, I almost thought you wouldn't."

I nodded, leaning my head back on her ratty seats, listening to Cherry chatter about everything she could think of, but my mind drifted.

Mom's shaking voice wormed its way into my brain, and I shook it out, trying to think of something good.

Like the way our hands fit together yesterday.

"Eryn?" Cherry said loudly, snapping her fingers as she stopped at a light.

"What?" I snapped, rubbing my eyes.

"Were you listening to anything I was saying?"

"Yep. Hanging on every word."

"What was the last thing I said?"

"Something about clothes."

She was quiet. "Wow," she said, drawing out the word. "You weren't listening at all."

"Yes I was!"

"Eryn, I was talking about planes." I winced. "How similar do you think clothes and planes are?"

I shrugged, crossing my arms.

"I bet I can guess what you were thinking about," she teased, wiggling her eyebrows.

I groaned and covered my eyes. This was going to be the longest car ride I have ever had the misfortune of being a part of. "Please don't."

"Hmm. Is it blond?" she asked, tapping her chin and pretending to think as I peeked at her from behind my fingers.

"Stop."

"I bet it's short too."

"How would you know?"

She looked over at my annoyed face and giggled. "Always wears a hoodie? I think your thoughts wear hoodies."

"I'm going to kill you."

"Shy?"

"You know what, I'll do you and myself a favor." I opened the car door as she sped up.

Cherry shrieked and lunged across me to pull the door shut with a resounding slam.

"Okay, okay!" She pretended to pout. "But I know I'm right."

"Cherry."

"Yeah I get it, shut up."

I rolled my eyes as she turned up the radio and started singing as loud as she could. She nudged me with her elbow, singing even louder and more obnoxiously when I laughed at her. Cherry threw her head back, practically screaming the words to her favorite song when she stopped at a light, and I couldn't help but join in, squeezing my eyes shut.

When we finally pulled into the Rainy Day Café, I was in a considerably better mood.

I jumped out as soon as she stopped, laughing as she groaned loudly.

I waited outside the back doors as Chery sighed, grabbing her apron from the back of the car, jerking her head towards the café.

I stepped inside, breathing in the smell of cold air and coffee. The walls echoed with the sound of Cherry slamming down her keys on the table.

I love this place most when it's empty. No one but Cherry and I, no one trying to talk to me or start awkward conversations.

I watched from my plush chair as she bustled around, checking supplies and pulling an apron over her clothes.

"Right," she sighed, plopping into the chair across from me, a few stray hairs falling from her bun. "Are you going to make this a thing?"

I blinked. "Make what a thing?"

"Pretending I have no idea who he is."

I huffed heavily. "I'm not, he's just, uh—"

"Shy?" She finished for me, a small smile on her face.

"Yeah."

"I get it."

She knew. I'm not surprised, Cherry just seems to know most things without me telling her about them. I would believe it if she told me she followed us yesterday, she's extremely sneaky.

"Love is a complicated thing."

"Whoa, what?"

She gave me a questioning look as she stood up to flip the closed sign to open and settling behind the counter.

"What?"

"We aren't in love."

The door swung open as two more employees came in, chatting cheerfully as they got ready.

"Not yet, but you will be, and the wedding's gonna be so cool!"

"Leave me alone," I said dramatically, flinging my arm over my face. "There will be no wedding."

"Are you saying you don't like him?"

"Stop putting words in my mouth Cherry."

"You're so boring!"

I shrugged from under my leather-clad arm. "Bring me coffee."

She stuck her tongue at me when I peeked out from

under my arm before smiling warmly at the customer who had walked in as we were talking.

The quiet of the mostly empty café slowly became a constant stream of quiet conversations. My eyes drooped despite my wishes, and I drifted off thinking of a flash of gold.

I woke to the incessant sound of Cherry's voice.

"Eryn, wake up!"

"What?" I asked, rubbing my eyes as I sat up.

"I should've brought you coffee earlier, huh?"

I nodded, taking the cup she held out, taking a careful sip.

"Someone's here by the way."

"There's a lot of people here, Cherry, are you talking about someone specific?" I asked, holding the cup close to my lips.

"You know who," she said, wiggling her shoulders.

I rolled my eyes, not caring enough to ask again.

Wait.

My eyes popped open and I sucked in a breath, inhaling coffee as I broke into a fit of coughing.

Cherry giggled as she pointed toward the corner of the café.

"Over there. Try not to hurt yourself."

I grunted as I took another sip, my eyes watering.

Cherry must have been trying to scare me or something. Parker wasn't in the corner where she had pointed, or anywhere in the café.

"Hi." I jumped at the sudden voice, spilling scalding hot coffee over my crotch, dropping the cup as I bit down on my lip as the pain set in.

The mug smashed against the ground into a million tiny pieces like my sanity as everyone in the café turned to look. People were quiet for a moment before they continued what they had been doing.

I tried to suppress my scream of pain.

"I'm so sorry, I thought you saw me," Parker said, taking his lilac jacket off.

He handed it to me, and I awkwardly held it for a moment before dabbing my jeans with it. It really wasn't doing anything to sop up the coffee, but I was grateful for the gesture.

"Eryn! I told you not to hurt yourself!" Cherry said from the register as one of her coworkers passed by her with a broom.

"I'm so sorry, I—"

"Parker, it's fine," I told him, smiling at his wide eyes and red face. "I just won't be able to have children. I'm happy to see you."

His smile was smaller than I'd hoped. "Me too."

He dropped to the floor to pick up larger pieces of the broken mug, ducking his head as his fingers deftly plucked glass from the floor.

"Hold on, you could hurt yourself," I said, wincing at my soggy jeans as I crouched beside him to help.

"I'm fine, I've done it a million times before."

"Dropped that many plates, huh?"

I could see his brows furrow even from my angle.

"Yeah."

Cherry's co-worker dropped the broom next to us, asking if we could clean it up before hurrying back to his station.

I stood up, handing Parker's jacket back. As he reached out to grab it, I noticed huge white bandages wrapping around his forearms.

"What happened?" I asked, trying to pull them closer.

"Nothing. It was my cat," Parker responded, his voice shrill.

"You have a cat?" He's never told me about a cat.

"Yeah. Isabelle." He glanced up at me before slipping the jacket back on.

"No, no, take that off. It's all wet, why would you put it back on?" He didn't answer me, instead picking up the broom.

"Here," I shrugged off my jacket, handing it to him.

He shook his head, stepping back. "No, it looks real and I don't want to—"

"Yeah, it's real and it feels great, try it on," I interrupted loudly, stepping closer.

Parker hesitated before leaning the broom against the wall and stepping closer still.

He ran his fingers through his thick hair and took off his sodden jacket, tossing it on the chair behind him.

I watched as he slipped my favorite jacket on. It was too big on him, covering the tips of fingers and heavy on his shoulders, but the way the brown looked against his blond hair made my heart drop like the floor had been ripped out from underneath me.

He looked up at me through his lashes, cheeks pink. The small smile that grew on his face was something I couldn't describe with only one word.

I've gotta re-evaluate what favorite means.

"How do I look?" he asked, spreading his arms.

"Amazing," I told him, shoving my hands in my pockets nervously. That word meant nothing compared to everything that he was.

I tore my eyes away, grabbing the broom and beginning to sweep up the glass, my mind racing.

He held the dustpan while I swept, our silence assuring our speed.

"All done!" I said, giving Parker a smile. He nodded, avoiding my gaze as he clutched the jacket around him tighter, like he thought it would fall off him and disappear.

We left the broom and trash bin by the chair as he stood nervously, and I went to ask Cherry for more coffee with a grin.

"You guys staying?" Cherry cooed, someone already making my previous order again.

"Yeah," I said, glancing to Parker who was still standing, picking at his nails.

"Good."

"Should I give him my jacket?" I asked suddenly, still watching Parker glance around nervously. His eyes kept landing on me and darting away. I was not going to leave;

didn't he understand that?

"No." I finally looked back at her. She looked mad, which surprised me.

"Why? It looks right on him, and besides, it feels right in a way."

"You barely know him. You love that jacket; you wear it constantly. Stop acting like a lovesick puppy, you have to keep it. It's yours," she hissed through her teeth, her face growing red.

I raised my hands, stepping out of the line. She needed to cool down, and I had better things to do than argue with her.

"I'll see you later. Give the coffee to someone else."

She nodded stiffly; her lips pursed angrily.

I made my way back to Parker, feeling Cherry's eyes burn holes into my back as I did. He looked up, his smile growing as I walked up, looking confused at my lack of coffee. He glanced behind me to Cherry, who was probably still watching us, and a look of quiet understanding washed over his face.

My leather hung from his broad shoulders perfectly, and I couldn't begin to describe how well it fit him even if I wanted to.

"Time to go?" he asked softly, tucking his phone into the jacket's pocket.

I nodded, gesturing in front of me, a smile growing on its own account when he nodded, ducking his head as he walked beneath the door frame, though he didn't need to. I followed him out, tuning out his repeated apologies.

Instead, I focused on the way his steps sounded, and the way he made plants seem brighter as he passed by.

The sky began to darken quicker as we walked, but I couldn't care less if it rained. I could already see the sidewalk peppered with the smallest drop of rain there could be, but when I glanced over to Parker, they clung to the strands of his hair fantastically.

He gestured as he spoke, his hands shaking the smallest bit, enough to make him hold them closer to his chest. I felt an urge like the one I had felt the first time I met him, I took one of them in my own, marveling at how perfect his hand fit mine.

I felt him flinch as I did, but he didn't pull away, so neither did I.

How strange it is, this feeling of content. With everything that happened last night, everything that happened this morning, I should not be feeling this, I should be at Cherry's, wallowing in how terrible my life was, but I was so glad that I wasn't in her bed. I was here, I was walking with Parker, I was holding his hand and feeling content with everything that was happening right now.

Mom said once she had felt content with Dad before things turned sour. If they had felt like this, I could understand Mom's haste to feel it again. It's truly an amazing feeling.

"Eryn?" Parker asked, his voice hesitant.

"Yep?"

"Where are we going?"

I shrugged, grinning at his exasperated expression. "Wherever the wind takes us."

He groaned, glancing around the street for a moment before fixing his brilliantly blue eyes on me.

"Can I pick?" he asked, his eyes sparkling.

"That's what I promised, right?"

He grinned, tugging on my hand as he started to run through the streets of Seattle, weaving through people as they headed towards wherever they were going.

Around this time of day, the streets were filled with tourists and locals alike, however, this is the time of year when it rains a lot, so most of the tourists are gone, waiting for sunnier days. Locals still pooled about, dressed in shorts and sweatshirts.

Parker glanced back at me, as if checking if the hand he was holding was still mine. I squeezed his hand tighter, and I watched as his cheeks turned pink. He squeezed mine and laughed, and I swear, people turned to look where this miraculous sound erupted from.

He suddenly ducked into a small alleyway, yanking me

behind the corner and sending me stumbling next to him. The noises of the city quieted as the sounds of Parker's and my own breathing filled the small space between us.

There was no one else here, and it was just wide enough to let Parker and I walk side by side.

Rain leaked down the walls to form puddles of the concrete, making every surface glint from the headlights of passing cars.

"This is...nice," I joked, looking around and nodding. "Do you come here often?"

"Shut up," he said, grinning at me. "C'mon."

We reached the end of the soaked alleyway and hurried right, away from the bustling city and down a separate pavement space behind all of the buildings.

Parker chuckled, seemingly at his own thoughts. It made me need to know how to make him do it again.

We reached an entrance to a large forest area, chest rising and falling rapidly.

"Why is this here? In the middle of Seattle of all places?" I asked, trying to catch my breath.

"They've been around for so long that the government doesn't want to get rid of them. They're part of the whole watershed thing."

"Oh."

He looked over, hair falling into his face, a thoughtful look in his eyes.

"It's pretty too. Good for tourists."

I nodded, practically hypnotized by that look.

He was watching me too, biting his lip in concentration. He was... fascinating in every way possible.

I suddenly realized I was leaning towards him. I jolted back, rubbing my now clammy palms on my jeans.

Out of the corner of my eyes, I saw Parker look down, grinning. I couldn't help but do the same.

"Now what?" I asked, clearing my throat.

Parker smiled and sprinted into the trees, looking angelic as he practically flew over the ground.

"Whoa, what?" I yelled, chasing after him.

He laughed, throwing his head back as raindrops showered his cheeks and hair.

I couldn't stop myself from feeling the happiest I've ever been. It seemed like Parker made me feel a lot of things I couldn't make myself feel.

I felt free, like running with him was the same as running with wolves. Was this what they felt? Did they chase after their brothers and sisters and feel this same feeling of freedom?

I wished I could run forever, feel my hair lift off my forehead and hear Parker's echoing laugh bouncing off passing trees.

We stopped at the edge of a massive tree, breathing hard. Its trunk was so big that it would've taken four of me to wrap my arms fully around it. Despite the daunting size, it truly was beautiful. There was a whole wall of leaves concealing the heart of the tree, and the rain, which had begun falling heavier without me noticing it, slid off the green and dripped into large puddles at the edge of the tree. I'm guessing the layers of leaves ensure the inside is mostly dry.

It sat alone in a small area void of other trees. Much taller trees reached far above it and covered the sky. The way they crossed over and twisting around each other almost made them look like arms.

Moss and ivy crept up the sides of the bark, and the wood was marked with dozens of carved initials.

Parker was staring up at the branches, his eyes slightly glazed over.

"Parks?" He turned to look at me, and I grinned at his expression. "Where the hell are we?"

"I-I thought you might want to see it, I mean. I practically grew up here, but I guess it's kind of weird to go on a date to a tree—"

"Wait," I started, leaning against the trunk, "What'd you call it?"

Parker bit his lip. "A tree."

"No, you said something else too," I told him, stepping closer.

His eyes avoided me while I waited for his answer. I liked how hard this was for him, I liked the fact that he liked me in his own quiet way.

"I uh, said it was a weird place to go on a date."

"Is that what this is?"

Parker turned towards the tree quickly, sucking his teeth loudly.

"Hopefully," he mumbled, his body casting a shadow as he stepped up to the tree.

Before I could say anything, he swung his leg up, hooking his foot into a notch of the wood and pulled himself up, the muscles in his back rippling.

I felt my breath waltz away as his body dangled for a moment before he pulled himself onto another thick branch, disappearing into a wall of green.

I stood shocked for a moment before he stuck his head out of the veil and grinned.

"C'mon! I could grow a beard waiting for you," he laughed, his eyes twinkling.

"Like you could grow a beard," I grumbled, trying to find the same footing Parker had.

"Shut up," he said, scrunching up his nose, crawling out again as he waited for me.

When I finally found the same slippery notch he has used, I swung myself up like he had, grunting as my muscles screamed.

"How did you do this so quick?" I groaned. Parker's laugh broke my feeble attempt at concentration, and I felt my hand slip.

For a moment, I felt time freeze as I looked up into Parker's panicked face, watching him as he began to lean forward.

Parker lunged for me, catching my wrist in his grasp, his arms shaking as he pulled me up to the branch he was on.

"You... are so... heavy," he complained.

"Rude," I grunted, struggling to pull myself up.

"I didn't mean—"

"Nah, it's fine, let me grab something."

I gripped his hand tighter, wrapping my arm around the wood next to his knee. With a grunt, I was on the branch next to him.

"How are you that strong?" I asked, breathing hard. "You're so small!"

I glared at Parker, who was giggling hysterically. "What?"

"You look like you almost died," he said, leaning back.

"I almost did! If you hadn't caught me, I would probably be bleeding out on the ground down there." I protested.

"Oh yeah, definitely," he said, rolling his eyes and brushing the wet hair that stuck to his freckled forehead away.

"You're my hero," I crooned, leaning close to him, grinning as his expression changed to one with wider eyes. He cleared his throat before gesturing behind me.

"Do you wanna head in?"

I nodded, throwing a wink in his direction before turning to crawl into the heart of the tree. He let out a strangled breath that was almost too quiet to hear, but I heard.

The wood was like glass under my hands, the outer layer worn down to a smooth and shiny light brown. The moss that thrived in the cracks and splits in the wood stained my hands green and made my knees wet.

I could hear Parker breathing behind me, and it was obvious even from his breathing that he had been crawling here for years.

I pulled the curtain of leaves as I crawled through, flinching as drops of rain fell from somewhere far above and rolled down my neck.

This part of the tree had branches so thick that I could probably sit comfortably without the fear of falling. There were small dents in the wood, probably from Parker eroding the wood over the years.

The leaves above layered each other, higher and higher

until I couldn't see the top layer, and just like I thought, the rain pattered against it, only letting a few drops worm their way through.

I made myself comfortable on one of the branches, leaning against them and watched Parker settle down as well.

"How often do you come here?" I asked.

"Almost every day. When I was younger, it was a safe place from... everything."

"Like what?"

He shook his head, staring down at his hands.

I started talking before I convinced myself otherwise, knowing that if I stopped, I would never continue, and I had to do this.

"Parks, can we try something?" I asked, leaning forward. I was so close that I could see the raindrops that had drenched even his eyebrows.

He jerked back, knocking his head against the wood before slowly leaning closer again, biting his lip.

"Um, okay?" he said cautiously, rubbing the back of his head.

"I want to know you better, but I don't know how without jabbing a sensitive subject, so let's just get those out of the way. You tell me something personal, and I'll tell you something personal. It's easy peasy."

"I don't know."

"Oh, come on," I said, scooching forward until our knees touched. Parker eyes our almost interlocking legs. "I know it's scary, believe me, I know, but it would be a cool way to get to know you. I've only known you for a couple days, but I really like you."

His eyebrows rose, his ears turning pink.

"You do?" he asked, his voice soft.

I nodded, feeling my own face grow slightly warmer.

"You're going first," Parker said, picking at his nails.

"Works for me," I said, watching him closely. He continued to stare at his hands.

"Where to start..." He snorted. "I guess I'll start with my

mom. I look just like her you know, the whole brown hair, same skin type, same build thing. She's much smaller than me though, and a lot prettier," I said, pulling a face, and Parker chuckled. "Um. But yeah, she's great. She says a lot of the same things over and over again, kinda like a mantra but also because they represent who she is, you know? She always said, 'it's one thing to be sad, but it's another thing to be unhealthy', for example. Man, she said that *all* the time. She doesn't say that anymore. I kinda think she doesn't believe it anymore." I looked up, staring up into the leaves that covered the dark grey sky. This was really hard, much harder than I had thought. "I love her to death. She divorced my dad when I was a kid, and I guess I was relieved, they fought all the time anyway, but it was still like losing my dad, you know?"

I let out a shaky breath, running my hand through my hair.

Parker slowly reached out with a trembling hand, taking my own and squeezing.

"He's gone now. Left town, deserted me and Mom. She remarried to this guy named Greg." I grit my teeth, looking down at Parker's hand. His nails were bitten down and uneven. I ran my thumb over the back of his hand. "He sucks. He's gross and rude, and he scares my mom all the time. It's not really just scaring, either, if you know what I mean... But she won't let me help. She's got these bruises on her cheekbone and shoulder that never seem to heal. And it's little things that make me more scared than anything. I mean, she never wore dresses when I was little, like *never*. She always said they made her uncomfortable, but she only wears dresses now. I know it was him. I keep trying to get her out of there, but she says he needs her." I refused to look up to his face. I didn't want to see how he reacted to this.

His palm was smooth, hardly any calluses, which was surprising, what with all the tree climbing he apparently does.

"The thing that sucks about it is that he does need her. He depends on her for food and for housework, cause he never does that any of that stuff. And he was a good guy when he first met my mom, but he was obviously faking it. He brought her roses and presents all the time, gave her fake compliments and stuff. I should've gone with my gut. I knew something was wrong with him." It suddenly felt much warmer in this small space.

"I dunno. I guess I could leave. I'm tired of seeing bruises on her. I don't like the bottles he leaves everywhere or the way he smalls or his inhumanly disgusting face or the way he breathes on us." It was getting hard to breathe, like stone was hardening around my throat. "Breathing the same air as him is bad enough, but when he reeks of booze..." I felt Parker twitch a bit, and I pulled his hand closer to me, forcing him to scoot closer.

"I can't leave her there, as much as I want to get away from him. One day, I'll get the both of us away." I chuckled bitterly. "I might have to kidnap my own mom."

Parker was silent. He didn't move as I turned his hand over and traced a thin silver scar on his pinky.

"I hate him. The bruises don't start to fade for weeks. My mom won't ever let me help her." Now I was repeating things. Time to move on before this gets worse. I cleared my throat.

"Cherry is really great. She pretty much knows everything, so I get out of the house and go to hers. My mom and her mom used to be really good friends, but my mom couldn't keep the connection."

I covered his warm hand with both of mine, keeping it dry from rebel drops of rain.

My chest aches. I don't want to continue, but his presence is enough to continue.

"And the diner too, I lived there. I knew the waitresses really well, and everyone there taught me about life when my mom couldn't."

I cleared my throat again, trying to force myself to speak, but all of my words seemed like they were too much for him to hear. I didn't want to scare him away.

Parker's hand was almost too warm in my grasp, but it made mine feel warm as well, so I took some comfort in that, in the warmth his body allowed me to keep.

I didn't say anything for a moment, and he didn't force me to. The sound of the rain hitting the ground around us was the only thing my racing mind needed to hear.

"My mom tried really hard, I don't want to make it seem like she didn't want to be there for me, she did, but she wasn't really allowed to help me grow up like she wanted to."

I pulled his knuckles to my chest, and he moved forward again, bending his arm slightly as he did.

I forced myself to look up, terrified I would find a horrified, disgusted look on his face.

He didn't look like he pitied me, and he didn't look disgusted. He just looked like he understood. I haven't seen that in a long time.

Not a lot of people understood this type of thing. Cherry understood the concept, and she was supportive, but she didn't suffer with me. Mom did of course, but she's too scared to talk. Too afraid of a man she could take without standing up.

She hasn't hugged me in a long time either, and I couldn't explain how much I miss the feel of her arms around me.

She used to tell me she believed in me every day, but I haven't heard anyone tell me that in years.

But Parker does. I know it. I can see straight to his soul through his deep blue eyes and I know it's perfect for me.

He was watching me, his white shirt sticking to his skin. His thick brows were furrowed, and his eyes slightly narrowed.

The rain made his hair stick to his forehead again, and our body heat made our shirts damp, but his hand was safe and dry from everything.

I leaned forward slightly, suddenly realizing our legs were tangled together, dangling from the tree that separated us from the world that refused to understand.

Parker leaned in slowly. Impossibly close. My eyes went cross-eyed trying to see him.

I could feel his hot breath on my lips. There was nothing in the world that would tear me away from him. All I wanted was him.

My hand cradled his cheek closer, and I leaned in closer.

A loud blaring noise made us both jump, shattering our moment.

Parker leaped back, breathing hard and running his hand through his wet hair.

I fumbled for my phone, nearly dropping it before accepting the call, feeling dizzy

"Hello?" I asked, breathless.

"Eryn? Where are you?

I narrowed my eyes. "Cherry."

"Yeah, it's me. Where are you? I got let off my shift super early, I was thinking we could make popcorn and watch a really bad movie at my place."

"What perfect timing," I said dryly.

"I know right? Are you coming?"

"One sec," I said, putting the call on mute, "Parker?"

He met my gaze, looking as dazed as I felt. "Do you wanna watch a movie with Cherry and me?"

He shook his head after a moment, his gaze never leaving mine. "No, I've got some homework to do."

"Oh. Okay." We were both quiet for a second.

My attention was brought back to Cherry as she loudly sang *Hey Brother*.

"Shut up! I'm coming," I told her, unmuting my phone.

"'Kay but hurry up." She hung up before waiting for a response.

The once comforting sound of rain on the leaves above us now whispered to me, telling me to break the silence.

"I'm sorry."

He cocked his head to the side. "Why?"

"I dunno. It was a lot, I guess. I get it if you're done with this whole dating thing or whatever," I said, rubbing the back of my neck.

"No, it was good." I snorted. "Seriously! No one's ever shared stuff like that with me before," he mumbled, squinting as he peered up.

"Well, I'm honored to be the first," I said, starting to get up. "Now you'll remember me."

"I would've remembered you anyway," he whispered.

His quiet confession sent warmth spreading through my chest.

"Uh, can I get your number? That way we can organize dates easier," I asked him, "We could talk more too, which is a plus."

"Oh," Parker said, his face turning red. "Sure, here."

He handed me his phone, and I quickly entered my number, my heart beating to the time of my fingers tapping out numbers.

"Text me in 15 minutes or something, okay?"

"Why 15 minutes?"

I grinned. "So, I'll know it's you."

He blushed as I left the hidden space in the tree, back into the shockingly cold rain.

Wait. I should've just sent a text immediately. Damnit! I'm ridiculously incompetent.

I practically fell out of the tree while scolding myself, my calves burning when I landed.

I peered back up at the tree, waving at Parker. I couldn't see him, but I hope he was able to see me.

I cursed Cherry as I ran to the edge of the forest, plunging myself back into the city.

Cherry was waiting for me in her car. I could tell without looking in that she was annoyed I was late, and honestly, I couldn't care less.

I knocked on the window, waiting for her to unlock it before I slid in quickly, suddenly realizing I was drenched.

"What the— why are you so wet?" She asked, shaking her head as she pulled her hair back into a low ponytail.

"I was out... walking... with Parker," I said, deciding not to tell her what we'd almost been doing.

"Really? I would've thought he was too wimpy for rain," she said, pulling the car into the busy road. "Like, I kinda see him freaking out over getting his hair wet or something."

"Why?" I asked, feeling personally offended.

"You know, he's just…" She shrugged.

"I really have no idea," I told her, crossing my arms.

"Shut up, he's just kinda all over the place. He talks too much."

I scoffed, my hair dripping water onto her seats.

"You can't tell me you don't agree." She chuckled, glancing over with playful eyes, but after everything that she had just interrupted, I wasn't in a playful mood.

I watched the colorful outfits of people and the grey of building pass by, knowing that she was getting more uneasy every uncomfortably quiet second that progressed.

"Here," Cherry said, tossing me a towel from her backseat. "Dry off, you're gonna make the seats moldy."

Good.

I flipped open the small mirror on the roof, sighing heavily.

My brown eyes stared back at me, narrowed and annoyed. My hair dripped water, following the length of my nose before falling.

Parker liked me. He liked me. My chest felt warmer, and I watched my reflection, wondering what part of me he would like best and which he would like the least.

I sighed and started drying my hair.

"You had fun though?" Cherry asked, sounding worried.

My lips twitched into a smile. "Yeah. I really did."

The rest of the drive was quiet, but it wasn't uncomfortable anymore.

As the dull buildings passed, the yellow raincoat someone was wearing reminded me of him, and so did the blue umbrella bobbing in the sky as the rain pattered onto it.

I flipped my phone over and over in my hand, turning the screen on every couple of minutes. This was torture. I could just text him new, but why would I do that? That's ridiculous, and ridiculous is not my middle name.

"You gave him your number, I'm guessing?" Cherry asked,

grinning at my impatient attitude.

"Yeah. He's gonna text me any minute now," I said, checking my notifications again.

"If you keep doing that it's gonna break," she said, snatching my phone out of my hands and tucking it under her leg. "There. Problem solved!"

"Cherry!" I whined, making her laugh.

I lunged for it, jump-scaring her in the process. She shrieked, jumping and jerking the wheel to the side for a split second before growling something under her breath, a smile on her face as she did.

"Eryn, don't! We're gonna die!" She laughed, pulling into her driveway and leaping out of the car, my phone in her grubby hands.

"Give it back, he said he was gonna text around now!" I yelled, running after her.

"Oh yeah sure, maybe he got tired of your bed head!" she teased, holding the phone above her head.

I was taller than her, I could've easily grabbed it from her awkwardly short arms, but I let her keep it. It's not like I would've been able to concentrate on grabbing it from her anyway.

I groaned, sitting on her front step and running my fingers through my still-damp hair.

"Cherry?" I asked quietly.

"Hmm?" She sat down next to me with a sigh, peering up into the dripping sky.

"I'm not crazy right?"

Cherry glanced over, sliding the phone back. I left it where it was on the porch.

"Why would you be?"

I didn't answer for a moment, trying to collect whatever thoughts had spilled out of those jars I kept in the back of my brain in Parker's presence. I had no idea what broke out, but now I was feeling things I had never felt before.

"I really like him," I said, quieter than before.

And I did. I didn't know I could feel like this for anyone. He makes my head spin and my heart felt lighter than I had ever been.

I don't remember when I had last felt hopeful for my future. And now, I see Parker's smile and I am so glad that I am alive in the same life as him, the same continent and time zone.

He's the absolute opposite of me, and yet his opposites filled in gaps I didn't know I could have ever been able to fill on my own.

I've never told her anything like this before. Four simple words, and I have never said them to her. Every guy she has ever pushed me into felt forced and fake, and I cannot explain how exhausted it made me feel every time some guy came up, asking if I knew Cherry, asking me if I wanted to go to dinner with him.

But Parker... he was a cup of coffee in a world without beds.

I didn't know if Cherry didn't know what to say or if she felt she didn't need to. I didn't ask.

She scooted closer to me until our bodies leaned against each other, and we listened to the rain that fell from the clouds so high above us hit the ground in silence, both stuck in our own worlds.

chapter eight
she called them orange poppies

I waited until I could no longer hear his footsteps before I fell against the branch, letting out a long breath.

My heart was still racing, and I almost felt like I wouldn't be able to breathe.

And still, the disappointment I had felt when his stupid phone rang still reared its ugly head.

I closed my eyes and tried to remember every detail of what had just happened.

When he'd first offered the idea, I had known I wouldn't be able to do it. I'm still surprised he went first. I kinda thought he only wanted to hear about me.

But he did. He talked about everything, his whole life story, his mom and his families, and the whole time, he had dug into his skin with his nails, refusing to look at me.

I had been worried he would hurt himself, and I'd felt a sudden rush of fear at the thought of blood welling over the skin of his finger, so I offered my hand. Better me than him.

He didn't do the same to me though. Maybe he didn't

even realize he had been close to breaking skin or that he'd been doing it at all, but he'd held mine like I was made of glass.

He had held my hand in his own, grazed over my fingers and palm in such a way that it seemed like he'd never seen someone else's hand before.

He was so honest.

His stepdad and mine.

I took another breath, not sure if I should cry or scream.

At home, the evening turned to night, and Mom didn't say goodnight. I should be used to it by now, but it still hurts my weak and pathetic soul.

I remained in my room, trying to stay quiet, slowly building up the courage to text him and hoping he wouldn't be upset by how long I had taken to respond.

I held my breath as I formulated response after response until I inevitably deleted all of them.

"I'm just gonna do it," I mumbled, typing 'hey' and sending it before I could stop myself.

I threw my phone to the end of the bed, feeling panicked at the thought of his face seeing my text and froze when it clattered to the ground loudly.

I covered my mouth and stifled my breathing as I strained my ears for footsteps.

After a minute, I slowly leaned over and picked my phone up, my heart still racing.

It buzzed immediately, making me jump.

Eryn: Hey! This parker?

For some reason my face felt hot as I said yes.

Eryn: Awesome!

Eryn: Wanna hang out tom?

He wanted to hang out? I felt overwhelmed already, the feeling of too much everything welling to my throat and gathering in a knot.

We had been together a couple hours ago, wasn't that enough? No one had ever wanted to hang out so much.

It's not enough. He wants more.

More of what? More of my clumsiness? My stammering and blushing? More of... me?

Parker: yeah, pick me up after school?

Eryn: Definitely.

I walked through the tightly packed crowd, very aware of my classmate's shoulders brushing against my own as they rushed to their cars, the bell signaling the end of a very long school day.

I felt a lump form in my throat as I started to pull myself out of the huddle of people, desperately trying to escape before something went wrong. After all, something always goes wrong in crowds.

"Hey!" I kept walking, hoping whoever was yelling wasn't talking to me.

"Hey! Parker! Wait up!" Of course they were talking to me, why wouldn't they be?

I stepped to the side, staring down at my shoes as I waited for them, my mind moving faster than my feet could ever run.

Loud footsteps pounded behind me, and I looked up, surprised to see Eryn grinning at me, breathing slightly harder than normal.

"Oh. You aren't who I thought you were," I told him, narrowing my eyes slightly. Why was he here?

"Who were you expecting?" he asked, nudging me towards the parking lot with his own shoulder. "You remembered we were hanging out today, right?" Oh. Crap.

"Uh, not really," I said, smiling sheepishly. "I mean, nobody really wants to walk with me, or hang out or anything," I gripped the straps of my backpack a bit tighter.

That achingly lonely voice in my head screamed, yelling at me to shut up before he left, shut up, shut up, shut—

"Really?" I shrugged. "Well, good thing they don't, otherwise, I wouldn't get the pleasure of your time," he said, smiling at me kindly. "You'd be swarmed with invitations to everything, and little ol' me would have nothing to do on this fine afternoon."

I felt my face warm. Who was this guy? Who gave me the right to feel this way?

As we reached Eryn's car, he stopped in the middle of the street, watching me strangely. He had this look on his face, one that hinted that he had an idea, an absolutely magnificent idea.

"What? What's wrong?" I asked, resting my hand on the hood of his car.

"Let's go somewhere."

"What, now?"

He nodded, beginning to back away from me, a smile growing on his face. I rushed after him, not wanting to be left alone in this huge and quickly emptying parking lot.

"Hold on! Where are we going? I asked, grabbing his arm to slow him down.

His leather jacket was soft and worn under my touch, and I couldn't shake the image of leather surrounding me, embracing me.

I dropped his arm, looking down nervously.

"I don't know. Let's walk until something catches our eye."

"So, we just keep walking?"

He nodded again, reaching down to take my hand in his own.

I pulled away without thinking, feeling an instantaneous wave of self-hatred wash over me. I watched as Eryn looked down at his feet, clenching his fists as his face turned the lightest shade of pink I have ever seen.

I was stupid, so unbelievably stupid, how could I continue to react like he was my father? He wasn't, he was the opposite of him, he—

"No! Wait," I grabbed Eryn's fist, interlocking our fingers when his grip loosened in surprise. "Sorry, I- I wasn't ready. But now uh, now I am."

Eryn's eyes were warm as he looked down at me, and he

pulled me closer to him as we left the school grounds.

We turned right, a way I had never gone before. As I looked back, Bersive High School disappeared behind the thickly grown trees.

The sun shone on us weakly as clouds threatened to cover it. I pressed my shoulder against Eryn as I felt the beginnings of cold creep down my neck, raking its fingernails down my back and legs.

"What's your favorite flower?" Eryn suddenly asked, tapping his leg absentmindedly with his free hand.

"Flower?" He nodded. "Uh, I don't really know, nobody's ever asked me that before."

"Alright, favorite color of flower, then."

"Orange."

"Hell yes. Mine's red."

I nodded, beginning to feel the start of a painfully awkward conversation.

"What do you like doing?" Eryn asked. I could hear the smile in his voice.

"You've already asked me that, idiot," I told him, poking his arm.

"Idiot? Ah! My poor wounded pride!" he exclaimed, clapping his hand over his heart and pretending to stumble. "Tell me again."

I fluffed my hair, trying to suppress my laughter. "I like reading."

"And?"

"And that's it."

"Oh, come on," he said loudly, shaking his head. "That can't be all. You're an interesting person! Do you draw? Write poetry? Debate?"

"Debate!" I laughed, amused at the very thought of me on a stage.

"Okay, you really expect me to believe you only study and read after school?"

"I mean, basically."

"Oh my God, thank goodness you know me, now you

have someone to do actually fun stuff with you."

I huffed, watching as the stores that we slowly passed by faded away into the distance.

"I do fun stuff," I mumbled, annoyed that he would assume I do nothing all day. I mean, he was right, but I was perfectly justified in my annoyance.

"Such as?"

I was quiet for a moment, but Eryn's snort caused me to blurt out whatever half-formed thought was in my head.

"I go to the café! And these, with you."

Eryn threw his free hand up. "Alright, fine! You are as experienced and fun as I am. You win."

I nodded, feeling satisfied.

"Look!" Eryn said, pointing at a sign in front of a shed that was painted a sky blue. It advertised an organic garden where people were able to pick their own vegetables, fruits, and herbs. There was a picture of a large, shiny apple on the sign, along with the bubble letters.

"A garden?" I thought we would go to another library, a different restaurant, but Eryn clearly had his heart set on the garden.

"Please? Like, the basket and all the fresh food would be so fun," he babbled excitedly, his eyes lit up and focused on the sign like a little kid in a candy store.

"I uh... I don't know if I can afford it," I mumbled, knowing for a fact that I couldn't.

Eryn's eyes moved to mine. I didn't think I'd ever get over how warm they appear, like if I held my hand over them my fingertips would smolder.

"I'll pay for you," he said matter-of-factly, striding towards the small shed, pulling me behind him.

"No, I can't ask you to do that again, I'll just wait for you out here—"

"No, you won't, it's boring out here, and besides, I want to be around you today," he told me, squeezing my hand encouragingly.

"But we... we hung out yesterday," I said, feeling my face

grow warm.

"One day is not enough, Princy," he said, slowing down for me as we drew closer to the entrance to the shed. "You're a mysterious person, and I want to know why."

I blinked, shocked into silence.

I'm not mysterious, I just don't like sharing my thoughts. At all. Does that make me mysterious? For wanting to keep the worst parts of myself out of the light?

He produces sentences like that as if they don't matter, like I already knew. He's confident in a way I don't understand. He's not arrogant, just... sure of himself in such a way that I am compelled to believe him.

I suppose I could be mysterious.

"I, uh... okay," I said, unable to formulate a more interesting sentence.

Eryn practically squealed in delight as the white gate surrounding the shed was in reach. He swung it open, holding it for me before closing it soundly behind us.

We knocked on the door at the same time, our knuckles bumping each other as we did, and a small, smooth voice called for us to come in.

There was an elderly woman at a small desk in front of us, sitting in a large rocking chair with a smile. The room around her was small, about the size of a garden shed, but it was wonderful. There were pictures covering the walls floor to ceiling, and the scent of fresh flowers hit me like a pleasant wave.

The woman had silver hair, and her wrinkled face looked friendly beyond belief. Her smile was bright as she welcomed us inside. I was immediately comforted by her presence.

"Hi there," she started, beginning to rock as she expertly began to sort hundreds of small brown seeds on a plate. "You two know how this works?"

"No, but we would love to," Eryn said while I shook my head silently in response.

She chuckled, her shoulders bouncing lightly. "It's nice to hear that some of you young people are still interested in plants. So, grab a basket," she gestured towards the small tower of what looked like hand-woven baskets beside her chair. "Pick whatever you'd like, and you pay for every five pounds when you're all done."

Eryn grinned at me, obviously ecstatic for his basket to be filled with her carefully grown fruit and vegetables.

"Thank you so much. Through here?" Eryn asked, pointing to a small metal door in the back of the cozy shed.

"Yes, sir. You two are the only people who have come by today, so enjoy the privacy!"

Eryn grabbed a basket from the pile, waiting for me as I grabbed one as well before he pulled me through the dark door.

Her garden was fantastic, something straight out of a storybook. Everything was green and plentiful, red tomatoes hanging heavily off thick green vines. There was a peach tree in the back, blooming with bright white flowers. Even with the heavy scents of herbs and the large squash next to me, I could smell the sweet scent of peaches leading me as I followed the bumpy cobblestone path.

I glanced at Eryn, who had already made his way over to a strawberry bush.

He looked back like he had felt my gaze, and I was suddenly struck with the way the bright red berries looked against his olive-colored skin, the way his lips stretched into a pleased smile, like I was all he needed to feel content.

He turned back to the plant, plucking the berries from their stems and carefully dropping them into his basket.

He was unlike anyone I have ever known. I mean look at this place! He brought me *here* when we could've gone anywhere else, and he brought me here? To a place of magic? How is it possible that she would've grown everything here all on her own? I wished I could just stay here with him.

"What'd you get?" Eryn suddenly asked, striding over to me, peering into my empty basket.

"Nothing. Haven't found anything I really want yet," I told him, feeling as though his eyes entrapped mine as he met my gaze. For once, I didn't feel the need to escape.

"Huh," was all he said. I felt my face warm as I stepped closer to him. He watched me, the smile slowly fading from his lips. His eyes flicked to my lips and back to my own eyes.

I wanted this. I wanted this moment more than I had ever wanted anything in my small life before, but I remembered the woman who was hidden just behind a thin door. I remembered Father, who would be livid if he found out.

I couldn't do this. I wanted everything, I wanted everything good this world could ever offer me so badly, but a voice in my head told me not to, screamed so loudly that I couldn't hear *my* own voice.

I remembered my father. He would've hated this; he would hate me more than he already does. Despite everything that has happened, I still desire his praise.

"Oh look," I said loudly, pretending to have spotted something behind him and hurried away from Eryn, my shoulder brushing against his gently. There was a burning feeling of longing that lingered there, and I rubbed it, hoping it would leave. It didn't.

When I glanced back, he was still standing where I had left him, blinking as though he was waking up.

I looked down to my arms, where the bandages were so white, they were blinding in the bright light that peeked through the clouds.

It was better this way. It had to be.

A spark of orange caught my eyes, and I looked around me to see a small part of the garden had been used to grow flowers.

They varied in every color, from blue to pink, and each one of them had their own little twist. The blue flowers had small dark spots near the center, the red flowers had streaks of white down the petals, the orange had round petals that looked like they were made of glass.

"Of course, you *would* find your way here," Eryn said from behind me, his footsteps quiet.

"What's that supposed to mean?" I asked, feeling a bit

defensive.

"To find the beauty," he simply said, and I felt my face grow even warmer.

"I mean, they're just flowers," I mumbled, reaching out to touch one of the delicate-looking petals of a bright yellow tulip.

"Flowers that you've found."

"Still flowers though."

Eryn sighed then, plucking one of the bright orange flowers and inspected it closely. He handed it to me after a moment, a small smile on his face.

"Still just a flower?"

I took it, feeling as though this flower was the only thing I would ever have to remember him.

He was right. It wasn't just a flower anymore. It was orange, my favorite color of flower, and this flower—this one flower in a garden full of everything one would ever need—was something Eryn knew would make me happy, so he gave it to me. Was that something a flower could do?

I shook my head, trying to shake off my slowly growing smile, placing it in my basket as I followed the wide path to the strawberries Eryn had been looking at earlier and began to pick them.

We were quiet for a while, the sound of vines snapping filling the air and disappearing into the sky.

"Parks! Look at this, you'll love it, I swear," Eryn exclaimed, waving me over.

I groaned when I saw what he was holding.

"Cilantro."

"Yes! And I know you adore cilantro," he said, wiggling his brows. "So, come here, take a big bite!"

"I will do no such thing," I told him, setting my basket down, knowing something was about to happen and started to back away from him.

"I think you will," Eryn said, stalking towards me.

"Get away from me, you monster!" I yelled, laughing as he tried to shove the leaves into my mouth.

"It's healthy! Fresh and delicious!" he yelled back, running after me through the garden, stumbling over the path as he did.

"I don't want it!"

"Yes you do!"

My foot suddenly caught a root that was exposed, and I fell forward, twisting quickly to land on my back heavily, knocking my breath from.

Eryn jumped at the chance, pinning my arms down with his knees as he dangled the herbs over my face.

"Eryn, stop, no!" I shrieked, gasping and struggling in vain as he laughed loudly.

"Fine, fine," he giggled, throwing the cilantro sprouts into his basket.

He stayed where he was. As in leaning over me with a soft smile that slowly disappeared from his face again as he took in my wide eyes.

You know. That kind of staying.

"Parks?" Eryn asked quietly, his hair hanging over his forehead.

"Yeah?" I would have winced at how hoarse my voice sounded, but the way he looked at me made me feel as though I had nothing to be ashamed of. The voice in the back of my mind reminded me

"Do you like it? The flower," he continued at my confused expression.

"I uh... yeah. I really do."

For a moment, I saw a fleck of the brightest orange I have ever seen in his eyes, but when I blinked, it disappeared. Like it had never existed.

In this garden, the soft noises of car engines faded away, and the light hit Eryn perfectly, making his face a silhouette.

And then, we heard a door begin to open.

Eryn jumped to his feet, pulling my outstretched hand up and practically flinging my nearly empty basket at me as he picked his heavy one up.

The woman hobbled over to us, holding the wooden

railing that lined the whole garden tightly as she smiled brilliantly at us.

"Find everything?" she asked a knowing look in her twinkling eyes.

"Oh yeah. This garden is amazing Ms...." Eryn trailed off, and I realized that we didn't actually know her name.

"Oh, call me Delores, honey," she chuckled, patting his shoulder as she peered into our baskets. "And I would hope so, I've only been growing this garden for nearly forty years. But thank you, dearie."

Delores clicked her tongue as she reached for my basket. I let her take it, feeling my face warm again as a flood of embarrassment washed over me.

"You need help, honey?" she asked me, her voice kind. "Sometimes, the good stuff needs an extra pair of hands to be found."

I nodded carefully, not willing to leave this place just yet.

Delores showed us around the garden, revealing fruits and vegetables we wouldn't have been able to find without her help.

She looked so deeply at home here, her freckled and wrinkled arms brushing leaves as she passed. Her thin hair was lifted up slightly as a breeze ran through her garden, and for a moment, it looked like the plants were reaching for her as a child reaches for their mother.

"Delores?" I found myself asking, uttering my first words to this female Pan.

She tilted her head towards me, her eyes trained on a slightly wilted leaf.

"Why do you do this? Grow this garden, I mean. This must take you hours to water them every day, and not only that, you—"

"Oh honey," she interrupted gently, smiling warmly at me. "Life is too short to worry about passing hours."

"What do you mean?" Eryn asked from behind me. I clutched my arms as I suddenly felt the warmth of him on my back.

"Well," Delores looked around her, holding her arms out graciously. "I enjoy this. I like the dirt under my nails, and I like the shade these plants provide in the summer. Why would I worry about what I'm doing in an hour when I enjoy doing this now?"

Eryn and I were silent, staring at Delores in wonder as she began making her way up the path, humming softly to herself.

"Well?" She asked, her fingers wrapped around the railings once more. "Are you boys coming? The day's fading, you know."

I glanced at Eryn finally, meeting his amazed eyes with my own.

"And you didn't want to come to a garden," he said, grabbing my hand and leading out of the garden Delores spent her life in.

As Delores rang us up, she commented on the variety Eryn had in his basket and the similarities in each of the fruits I had decided to pick.

When she picked up my crumpled flower from the bottom of the basket, she smiled fondly, looking up at us with another of her knowing gazes.

"What are your names?" she asked us.

"Parker," I told her softly.

"And Eryn," Eryn said, squeezing my hand.

"Well, Eryn and Parker, I enjoyed your company today quite a bit, and so I will gift you with a sprout of this flower," she told us, standing up with a heavy sigh. She hurried into her kitchen, mumbling to herself as she picked up a large pot with a small green sprout poking out of the dark dirt.

"Oh no, I couldn't," I told her, shaking my head. "I don't have money right now, but I'll pay you back later—"

"It's not a gift if you pay for it," Delores said, handing Eryn the receipt for our baskets. "And you have already paid for your food. Take it. Please."

I nodded, taking the heavy pot from her hands, juggling the bag that carried all of the fruit I had picked.

"Water her once every couple of days," she said,

waggling her pointed index finger at me. "She's an orange poppy, so she blooms soon. Take care of her, alright?"

I nodded again, looking around her small shed one last time as Eryn said his goodbyes.

My eyes stopped on a small framed picture on a small shelf. It was from a very long time ago, but it was obviously Delores. There was another woman in the picture. Both wore white dresses, and the other woman wore a small white veil. Dolores was grinning, holding a bouquet of orange poppies— the same flowers that Eryn had picked for me—while the other woman kissed Delores' cheek. They both looked blissful.

"Ready?" Eryn asked me, a small smile growing on his face.

I felt dazed from the events of the day, but his voice grounded me like an anchor.

"Yeah." This time, I reached for his hand, smiling when he looked down in surprise.

"Oh, and boys?" We both turned at the sound of her voice. "Take care of yourselves, alright?"

"We will, ma'am."

She smiled as we walked out, and all at once, I was reminded that her world was not mine as the cars zoomed by too fast for their own good.

She was happy, and she knew what the world could offer, and I... didn't.

I was a balloon, flying higher and higher until in one moment—just one moment—I pop.

Eryn drove me home, talking about how excited his mom was going to be to see all the fresh food in their fridge.

I thought of my father's face, the way Mom's nose will wrinkle at the sight of the dirty pot in my room, the cups of water that I will bring in to water it.

I wonder just how much it would hurt if the pot was thrown at me.

Eryn dropped me off a block away from my home again, right by the mailbox. He waved goodbye, and just like before,

I waited until I could no longer see the lights of his car before beginning to walk home.

When I reached my front door, I pressed my ear against the wood, shifting the flower's weight in my arms.

Nothing. I glanced to the driveway, checking to see if Father's truck was home before opening the door slowly.

The house was silent. I crept through my own house like a thief, placing the fruits I had collected in the fridge and rushed upstairs, grunting under the combined weight of my backpack and the heavy flowerpot.

Once my bedroom door was closed, I placed the pot on the windowsill, turning it until the light from the moon hit it perfectly.

For the rest of the night, I stayed awake, watching the orange poppy grow so slowly that I couldn't tell a difference in the plant, but it didn't matter.

I was waiting for the fleck of orange.

"Hey! Parky!"

I looked up from my textbooks, my pencil paused as I waited for whoever was talking to me.

The huge bulky figure of Brett Gray stood in front of my desk; his tan face twisted into a sneer.

"Whatcha doin'? Looking up how to find the nearest cliff?" He laughed loudly and the girls next to me tittered, grinning at Brett.

"In a textbook?" I asked quietly, looking down at the diagrams spread across the pages.

"What'd you say?" he asked, squaring his shoulders as he stared down at me.

"Nothing," I whispered, wishing I could disappear.

"That's what I thought."

I shook my head, trying to get back to work as the teacher barked instructions, something Brett had never listened to and he wouldn't start today.

"Say Parky— you don't mind if I call you Parky, do you?" he asked.

"Actually, I—"

"Here's the thing Parky," he interrupted. "You're always sitting in my seat, and I'm getting kinda pissed off. Wanna know why that seat's mine?"

"You've never sat here before."

"Sorry, did you guys hear that?" he asked the group of guys behind him, smirking. "Sounds like a bug or something."

"Listen, I'll just move my stuff, you can sit here—"

"Actually, Parky, I was asking you a question, and you should wait until I say it, got it?" I flinched at the sound of his loud voice, and nodded, holding my books close to my chest. "Wanna know why that seat is mine?" He leaned in, whispering in my ear. "Because you're sitting in it."

"What? Then all of the seats I sit in will be your seat!" I protested, backing my chair up slowly.

"Finally got it, didn't you? There's really no way out, is there?"

"I don't understand what you want me to do," I whispered.

"Of course you don't. Because you're weak right?" he said, crouching beside my desk. "Say it."

"What?" I asked, looking up at Brett's narrowed eyes, glinting like obsidian.

He was too close, way too close. I could feel my heart speeding up.

"Say it. You're weak and a teacher's pet."

"N-no!" I said, standing up, my eyes searching for an escape.

His huge hand slammed down on my shoulder, shoving me back down into my chair. My leg twisted roughly under my sudden weight, and I bit back a yelp. His now towering figure bent down to stare menacingly at me.

"Say it, or I'll beat you in front of the class," he whispered, all traces of amusement suddenly gone.

My head filled with the ear-shattering sound of my shallow breathing, and my legs twitched. I didn't want to do anything he told me to, I wanted to go home.

"Say it."

"Who are you?"

Brett looked behind him at the door where Eryn's frame filled the empty door frame.

Where the hell did he come from? He has to go; he's only going to make this worse for us. I could already feel my panic rising as Eryn stared Brett down.

"Who wants to know?" Brett asked, straightening to his full height.

"I do. Who. Are. You." Eryn demanded; his voice stony.

"Brett," he answered, grinning. He thought this was a joke, he really did.

"Great," Eryn glanced at me, his gaze softening for a moment before landing on Brett like a missile. "So, what are you doing?"

"Hear that, Parky?" Brett said loudly. "Your little boyfriend came to your rescue! So sad you can't save yourself, but then again, only people like me are able to save themselves. You're too weak and pathetic."

Oh, how right he was. If only he knew how true every word was.

"Excuse you, I'm talking to you," Eryn said, stalking closer to him, nearly a full two inches taller than Brett. "What do you want from him?"

Brett looked back at me, cold amusement shrouding his eyes. "Nothing much. I just wanna hang out with my new punching bag."

I stood up quickly, my body moving without direction, gathering my bag and books that I had been gripping tightly.

He strode towards me, grabbing my shoulder and squeezing painfully.

"Where ya going?" he asked, the girl's sneers now focused on me. Why weren't they helping me?

"I fee-feel sick, I have to go," I mumbled before Brett slammed the books out of my hands. They clattered across the floor, spilling every paper I had kept inside everywhere. They flew across the ground like birds soaring in the wind, and

I ached to join them.

"Oh no, you feel just fine." He pulled his fist back and punched me in the stomach, and all at once, knocking every ounce of oxygen out of me.

I crumpled to the floor, my eyes watering, gasping, wanting this to end no matter the cost. Birds were not worth this.

The class was in uproar, screaming and cheering, and I squeezed my eyes shut, preparing to be kicked like all the other times this had happened.

A loud crash forced my eyes open, and I blinked a few times to see Brett on the floor surrounded my overturned desks and chairs.

Now the teacher suddenly stood up, yelling something that I couldn't hear.

Eryn ignored her, picking Brett up by the collar of his shirt and pinning him against the wall.

I didn't know he was this strong, but he just picked up a two-hundred-something pound guy and tossed him around effortlessly.

Eryn leaned in like he was whispering in his ear, and Brett's eyes widened, and he nodded quickly, his face bright red.

Eryn dropped him, and Brett fell to the floor, gasping like I had been moments ago. I grabbed all my stuff, holding my breath as a now dull pain rippled through my stomach and fled the classroom, running as fast as I could.

I blinked hard to stop the tears that stung my eyes from falling.

As I reached the nurse's office, the nurse looked up from her computer with a bored look on her face.

"I need to go home, I'm getting a migraine," I mumbled, still blinking rapidly.

"Do you have your parking pass with you?"

"No, but I have my I.D—"

"No pass, no way home without a parent's signature."

"But I—"

"I have my pass."

I refused to look at Eryn as the nurse took his pass, peering suspiciously at us.

"Why do you need to leave?"

"I'm his ride. His parents are at work and I promised I'd take him home if something like this happened."

She sighed and nodded, handing me a hall pass and giving Eryn his parking pass back.

"Hope you feel better."

I nodded as I rushed through the front doors, clutching my backpack to my chest.

"Parker!" Eryn yelled. "Hold on!"

The cold air rushed into my lungs, burning my throat as I ran across the parking lot, not caring enough to check for cars. I could still hear Eryn yelling for me, but I couldn't *hear* him. I only heard the rushing air, the sound of my heavy breathing, and my feet pounding the ground.

I finally stopped beside his car, pressing the heel of my palm into my eye, demanding myself not to cry in front of him.

When Eryn reached me, he no longer said anything, only unlocking my side and waiting for me to get in before starting the car.

I turned to the window, suddenly realizing how tight I was gripping the backpack. I tightened my fists.

Eryn pulled out of the parking lot, turning away from the street I usually went down. I said nothing, not trusting myself to speak without breaking down.

He didn't turn on music, and I was grateful for the silence. My swirling head couldn't take much more.

The trees got thicker the longer we drove, and I saw fewer and fewer cars on the road. Still, I didn't care. I wouldn't have cared if a car barreled towards us and hit my side if Eryn lived.

That's the funny thing about life. It's gone so soon. I could jump off a cliff right now with a stretchy rope tied around my waist and live, but if one mechanical machine hit my side of the car, I would die. Eryn probably wouldn't, but there was still a chance, so did I really want to take it?

I glanced at him, blinking profusely. He stared straight ahead, focused on nothing and everything all at once. I knew he saw me watching him; his brow furrowed a little more as I did, but he didn't say a word.

No. I suppose I wouldn't.

Eryn took a sharp left, forcing me to drop my heavy backpack onto the floor of the car, and pulled into a dead end. I clenched my fists, feeling my nails dig into my palms.

We were at the edge of a forest, in a small parking space big enough for one car that was almost hidden by branches and overgrown grass. It felt too small and too big all at once, and I didn't know how to fix that.

Eryn shut off the car, and suddenly, the silence was deafening.

"Parker—"

I whipped my body around in the seat and wrapped my arms around his torso, so close to crying I was shaking.

I pressed my face into his chest, hoping he couldn't see my face. He somehow still smelled like leather without his jacket, the same jacket that hung from my shoulders now. I was suddenly very aware of it, the way it creased as I clutched him, the way it smelled like him: leather and clean laundry.

After a moment, Eryn's arms enveloped me, pulling me closer.

The console was digging into my stomach and my back was bent awkwardly as I leaned over it, but I wasn't about to move. Not now, maybe not ever.

Eryn's hand rubbed my back in soothing circles.

"It's gonna be okay," he whispered, and with that, I deflated.

Tears seeped out of my eyes even when they were closed, and I sobbed loudly as Eryn squeezed me tighter. The sound of them felt so loud in the confines of his ugly green car. They were closing in, weren't they, the sound of them so loud, the feeling of my body shaking against Eryn's still one.

I felt awful. My tears were soaking Eryn's shirt, my nose

was running, and I was humiliated, but I can't stop myself from practically choking on my wracking sobs.

Eryn's arms didn't falter. Neither did his hand or his voice, telling me it would be okay, that he was here for me.

For once in my awful, worthless life, I felt safe.

"Do you need me to call anyone?" Eryn asked, gently holding my head to his chest as I continued to lean on him.

I didn't know how long it had been since I had begun to cry, but it had been a very long time until I was able to stop.

I shook my head, "No one to call."

"Your parents?"

I shook my head again.

He sucked his teeth and held me tighter. "Well, at the very least, you have me," he said, rubbing my back.

The very least? At the moment, he was everything I needed to feel.

"Thank you, Eryn."

I felt him let out a little breath.

"Parks?" I smiled at the nickname.

"Yeah?"

"I like you."

"I would hope so, this would've been really awkward, especially after all those dates."

"You're making jokes? You were just crying!"

I shrugged.

"But you know that, right?" he asked, his voice suddenly serious.

"Know what?"

"That I like you. That I enjoy your existence."

"I know now." Something pushed against my heart, against the ache in my throat. I had to say it back. I had to, when would I get a better chance than this? "I like you too," I whispered.

Eryn was quiet for a moment.

"You know the jacket I gave you?"

I laughed wetly. "The one you let me borrow because I

dumped coffee all over you?"

"You scared me, and I dumped coffee on *myself*."

"Yeah, that's a huge difference."

His deep chuckles bounced my head a little.

"It was my grandpa's," he said quietly.

I shifted my body to lean my head against his shoulder and reached to take his hand. My own hands were still shaking, but I stroked the back of his hand with my thumb, the jacket making a soft crumpling noise as I moved.

"It looked great on him. He looked like an old detective. He swore it gave him powers 'til the day he died. He said it gave him the bravery to talk to my grandma. He uh, he always said she was so beautiful that he melted every time he looked at her. He wore it to her funeral. He wore it on my birthday and when my parents divorced. He wore it when he went to the hospital. He told me that if I needed to be brave, wear it. After he died, I wore it every day."

After a moment, my eyes stinging with hot tears once more, I asked, "Why would you let me wear it?"

"Every time I saw you, you looked terrified. I just wanted to make you happy." I heard a smile in his voice. "Maybe the jacket makes you brave, maybe it doesn't, but you look damn good in it, so that helps too."

I laughed through tears.

"I... I feel brave when I'm with you." I never realized it until I said it, but it's true.

"I'm glad. You make me brave, too," he said.

In this car, this ugly green car surrounded by the smell of leather, protected from dark skies and rain, Eryn held me, and I held him.

It was safe.

He drove me home twenty minutes after school for everyone else ended, holding my hand the whole time.

"I'm sorry we didn't go on a date," I said after he parked a block away.

"Eh, we've got time for another," he said, eyes crinkling. "The whole world will wait for us! Stay safe."

I nodded, getting out of the car.

He waved, making a goofy face.

I waved back as he drove away, and I watched his lights disappear.

When I returned home, I head a baseball game blaring through the windows.

It got much louder when I opened the door and Father yelled something at the TV.

"Why are you home so early," Father demanded, taking a swig from his beer.

"I got a ride," I said quietly, closing the door behind me.

"From who? You don't have any friends. Not someone like you."

I bit my lip. "Someone felt bad for me."

"Oh sure," he said loudly. "You probably did a little something to convince them." He turned back to his game, completely ignoring my existence.

I stopped for a second, feeling utterly useless and digging my nails into the skin of my hands. Nothing I could say would make him believe me. Nothing I could say would prove to him that I wasn't the person he thought I was. I haven't said anything like that to him, haven't tried to convince him that I was worthy of him. He hates me.

I carefully made my way up the stairs and closed my own door softly.

I turned around slowly, staring at my whole life plastered onto these walls. I felt my muscles lock as I stood.

My teeth started chattering.

He hates me. He hates me, *why* does he have to hate me? I trusted him, I loved him! The hardest part of all this crap is that I did love him once, and I remember loving him. I still need his praise, he's my father for God's sake!

I thought he loved me too, I mean, I'm only his son. Why should it matter who I like? Why does it matter so much to him? Is it just because it's me that like men and not someone else?

What's wrong with me? Why can't I be enough for him?

My knees locked and I fell to the ground, heart beating like I had run a mile.

Mom doesn't love me either. She insists she does, but she refused to put me first, to love me first, and that hurt more than the knowledge that Father doesn't.

They were the ones who decided to have me! Why would they hate the thing they created so much, why did they decide to put me through this misery in the first place when they could've made sure I never existed?

I grabbed my phone, hands shaking. The dial tone was so loud in my ears that my brain felt like it was going to explode, and I would've screamed if I wasn't so out of breath.

"Hello?" Eryn's tinny voice said in my ear, an anchor in an ocean terrorized by storms. "Parks? Are you okay?"

I couldn't respond. My mind was racing so fast that I couldn't hear him properly.

"What the— what's happening?"

I tried to answer him, but my throat constricted my words, my chest rising and falling in broken breaths.

"Hey, hey, it's okay, everything is fine," he soothed, probably hearing my gasps.

I shouldn't have called him. I couldn't believe how humiliated I was. I've done this alone countless times and I should've done it alone this time.

What's the point anyway? If I disappeared, how long would it take for people to forget me? Would anyone even notice I'm gone?

I don't want to be forgotten.

Oh God. Father would never love me. He would never invite me to Thanksgiving dinner when I get older, he would never visit me in college, he would never give me advice on how to ask out my crush. How could he not love me?

"No, just—" My jaw was clenched so hard it ached. "Keep talking, I-I-I-I—"

"Okay, it's gonna be okay," he said. I could hear the worry in his voice.

"I'm sorry. God, I'm sorry, I shouldn't have called, I shouldn't have scared you, especially after everything I did today," I rambled, closing my eyes and trying to stop the white flashes that flickered across my eyes like static.

"No, I'm glad you did, I'm here to help. I'm your boyfriend, of course I care."

Damnit. How dare he say that to me; how dare he be nicer to me than my own parents.

"Thank you," I mumbled through shaking lips.

"Of course. Wait!" he suddenly said, "Don't hang up! I could—"

"I'm not going to, just stop asking stuff, just keep talking," I said quickly. "I don't— I don't—" I groaned. "I don't want to think," I held my head between my knees to stop myself from throwing up.

"You want a story?"

"Anything."

"Okay," he cleared his throat before starting. "Um, once upon a time, there was a handsome prince." He laughed awkwardly. "He was loved dearly by the kingdom. There wasn't a person who hated him in all the lands. I mean, there was one."

He was quiet for a moment.

"There was an evil wizard, a real ugly one, like super nasty. He heated the prince because the people loved him instead of this wizard."

Broken thoughts of being part of a tribe of lost people whipped through my mind like a snowstorm of panic.

"So, he made a potion, put it in a small cake thing and gave it to the prince on a celebration day. The prince loved his people and trusted them, so he ate it gratefully. As the kingdom watched, the prince smiled and exploded."

"What?" I asked, trying to laugh through tight muscles.

"Yeah. He exploded into scales, and suddenly, he was this huge dragon—"

"That's different than actually exploding."

"Oh, I'm sorry Mr. Factual, do you want a story or not?"

I stopped thinking, forcing myself to listen.

"So, as I was saying, the kingdom panicked. Their beloved prince was gone, and a terrifying dragon was in his place. Naturally, they tried to kill it. They thought it had eaten their prince, of course they would try to kill it! The prince, disguised as the dragon, escaped and fled to a mountain, in a cave where he thought no one could find him."

I almost couldn't keep listening. Exhaustion was at my door, knocking loudly. I almost felt okay again, but I still forced myself to listen, forced myself to shove back those thoughts of fear.

"But a man, a peasant, had been watching the prince for a long time, wanting to keep him safe. He followed the dragon's trail, knowing that this dragon was the prince. People warned him of the dangers that he would have to endure, but he didn't listen because he didn't care. When he found where the dragon was hiding, he gathered his courage and dropped all his weapons and armor."

"He's gonna die."

"Shut up! The dragon didn't do anything when the peasant walked in. It just kept its head low and watched him with yellow eyes. Maybe the dragon wanted to die."

Something panged in my chest, my heart leaping into my throat.

"What do you mean?" I asked, trying to keep my breathing slow.

"Well, he thought the townspeople hated him. They didn't, they just thought the dragon ate him. But the prince didn't know that. They were mad and scared at the monster that he had been transformed into. He had never felt anything but love, because he was a good person, ya know?"

I nodded before realizing he couldn't see it. "Yeah."

"So anyway, the peasant walked in, vulnerable, but the dragon didn't do anything. The peasant goes up to him and asks him if he was alright. The dragon just closed his eyes."

Eryn's voice lulled me into a light sleep; I could hear his words, but I didn't process them. For the second time today, I felt safe, except this time, I was in my own home.

"The peasant pulled out an antidote and gave it to the dragon. It turned him back into a prince with blond hair. The prince asked what he could do to repay him. The peasant just... he just asked the prince to love him."

I fell into a deep sleep, my mind and body drained.

When I woke up, my phone was scalding hot against my cheek. I blinked blurry sleep from my eyes and stretched my sore, stiff shoulders.

I glanced down at my phone, shocked to see that I was still on the call with Eryn.

We had been calling each other for so long my phone was almost dead. It was amazing that it hadn't already died.

I pressed the hot screen to my cheek again cautiously. I could faintly hear his breathing, and I felt my heart flutter.

I wonder what he would look like asleep. Would he snore? Usually I hated it when people snored, but I don't think I would mind if he did.

I tried not to imagine his bedhead, feeling my face grow warm as I failed miserably.

I sighed, leaning against my wall and feeling a small smile grow of its own accord.

He sighed loudly, mumbling something too quiet for me to hear. I panicked, ending the call quickly. My hands felt like they were vibrating, so I grabbed my elbows to steady myself.

I started at the feel of the bandages wrapped around my arms.

Nothing happened last night, because Eryn was telling his story. I felt bad for not hearing the ending, but his voice has been so soothing. I can't remember the last time I had fallen asleep peacefully.

But today has its own challenges, and I must be quick to face them.

First challenge: get out of the house before anyone notices.

The café is a place I have stopped by more than my own house lately.

Being with Eryn for this long was scary, if I was being honest. He always wanted to know about me, what I liked, what I believed in, but I have always been too scared to share.

It's not that I didn't want to, it's just that I couldn't. I have nowhere else to live, so I'd rather just stay quiet.

Today, Cherry asked Eryn to cover her shift so she could finish an essay, so naturally, I was already on my way there when I saw them.

It's strangely lonely watching them interact. They've obviously been friends for a long time, and it showed in the way they acted around each other.

As we walked into the Rainy Day Café, Eryn casually slung his arm around my hips, and strangely, I really liked the heavy feel of his arm pressing down on me.

I watched as an older man turned to grumble at his wife, his narrowed eyes directed at me.

My face burned as I pushed Eryn's arm off me.

"What, don't want my diseased arm on you?" Eryn asked, leaning closer to kiss my forehead.

I ducked before he could, shuffling over to our corner. "Ugh, of course not, you're gross," I tried to tease, my smile weak.

Eryn grinned at me as he headed into the back to get ready for the day.

Cherry sat down next to me, pulling her laptop out of her bag, smiling politely at me. I'd almost forgotten she had been walking beside us. It made me uneasy that she had been so quiet, since usually she has a very loud presence.

I smiled back, settling down with my book as she turned back to her screen.

We were both silent, both focused on each of our self-assigned tasks.

"What do you want from this relationship?" she asked

turning quickly to face me and startling me in the process.

"Sorry?" I asked, trying to process what she had said.

"What do you want from him?"

I felt put on the spot, my heart suddenly racing.

"I just like him, I guess." I laughed awkwardly. "He makes me happy."

"Do you actually like him?" she asked bluntly, crossing her legs as she pulled her armchair closer to mine.

"What?"

"Is that a no?"

"No! I mean, no it's not a no, why would you ask me that?" I asked, feeling incredibly nervous.

"Because if you're leading him on because you want something, you'll not only break him, but you'll have me to answer to," she said, her face stony.

"Cherry, I'm not leading him on. I... I really do like him." I said quietly, staring at my hands. What a ridiculous thing to be embarrassed of.

"Huh," Cherry said, making me look up.

"What?"

"Eryn said the same thing about you."

I felt my face grow warmer, and my heart fluttered.

"You wear his jacket all the time now," she stated. Her eyes weren't unkind as she spoke, but with her hair up, she looked more serious, and that did make me nervous.

"He said I could. I tried to give it back, I swear."

"Parker, can I ask you something?"

She was changing topics too quickly. I felt dizzy.

"Uh... sure?"

"Do you have depression?"

"What?" I asked, reeling.

"It's okay if you do, I do too. Do you?"

I shook my head, glancing out the window. "I don't know."

Depression was a very strong word, and I wasn't all that strong. I wasn't the worst case, of that I was sure, so there's no point calling whatever this is depression. It couldn't be. I've never been to a therapist, so that must mean I'm fine, right? Even when I'm tempted to do something I might regret, that must just be growing up, right? Right?

"I think you might," Cherry said, pulling out lip balm and applying it generously before sliding it back into her bag. "I'm not saying this to be rude either, but it's not just about you."

"What?"

"Your relationship with Eryn. It's not all about you."

"I know that," I said, feeling defensive.

"Depression is really hard, I would know that better than anyone," she said, resting her hand on the back of my chair as she leaned a little closer. "But you can't let it control your life. You just can't."

"Who says I'm depressed?" I asked, crossing my arms and leaning back from her.

She looked at me with a sad smile. "I'm sorry. I was too forward?"

I nodded awkwardly, hoping this wouldn't lead her down another path.

"Ugh!" She leaned back in her chair, covering her face dramatically. "Sorry, Eryn usually stops me with this kind of stuff, I'm not the best with people."

I nodded again, feeling relieved that she was done talking about depression and still feeling deeply uncomfortable.

"Um, let's talk about something else," she said, glancing back to the counter and holding two fingers up.

Eryn nodded and flipped her off.

"Jerk," she mumbled, grinning. "So. Whatcha reading?"

I glanced down at the book cover. I've read it a million times throughout my life, it's always been my favorite. It's always been the first book I picked up when something went wrong.

"Uh, it's an action book," I said quietly, pulling Eryn's leather jacket around me closer.

Cherry's brows shot up. "Really? Is it gory?"

"Um, relatively gory I guess."

"I didn't think you'd be into that kind of stuff."

I shrugged. "Yeah, I get it."

"You're just so cute."

"I'm not cute."

"Yes, you are! The cutest guy ever!" she teased, poking my arm.

I felt strange. I didn't usually get a ton of attention. Well, Eryn gave me a lot, I suppose, but he didn't count. He was my boyfriend, after all. I couldn't tell if she made me uncomfortable or if it's just normal.

"Not cute, just gross," I said, ruffling my hair.

"No," she responded, drawing out the word as she pulled her legs onto the chair and crossed them. "Maybe you don't think you're as cute as everyone says, but Eryn likes you for a reason." She winked.

I felt my face grow hot as Eryn walked over, holding two cups that smelled amazing.

"One black coffee for Cherry," he said, bowing as he handed her a steaming mug. "And one mocha for my prince."

I took it from his hand, trying to ignore Cherry's smirk. I hope she doesn't make this weird.

"So!" Eryn said, crossing his arms. "What are you guys talking about?"

"You," Cherry said, grinning at my attempt of drinking coffee in order to avoid explaining and burning my throat in the process. "I've decided to accept your relationship. You have my blessing." She made it weird.

Eryn's eyes lit up. "You like us?"

"Yeah."

Eryn grinned, pulling me up from my chair and crushing me against his chest in a triumphant hug.

"Parks! We no longer have to date in secret! The fear has been vanquished!"

"I wasn't," I said, blushing even harder at Cherry's small smile at the nickname. "Get off me, you're so warm!"

"You like my warm!"

Yeah, but not right now, you're too warm."

"Fine, I have to go back to work anyway," he said, kissing

the top of my head before waving to Cherry and going back to the register.

"Yeah," she said, watching me gulp coffee to hide my red face. "You guys are good together."

chapter nine
hair like gold

Eryn

I walked through the front doors of the school, yawning as classmates squeezed in around me, yelling and complaining.

"Parker, don't you have anything else to wear?" Cherry's voice carried across the hallway.

I walked faster, realizing that Cherry and Parker must have arrived at my locker at the same time. This was gonna be weird.

When I finally got there, Parker looked deeply uncomfortable as Cherry talked about his poor fashion choices.

Cherry stood in front of him, scrutinizing his light green jacket and jeans, a frown on her usually cheery face.

His searching eyes landed on mine, and I watched as his hands calmed considerably from the frenzied wringing he had been doing. It warmed my heart to know that I really did make him brave.

"Hey Cherry, how's life?" I asked, bumping knuckles with her before moving next to Parker, winking at him as I did.

Today, she was wearing a checkered overshirt (most likely one that she had found at a thrift shop) over a crop top and skinny jeans. She looked like a supermodel next to Parker, but my heart still fluttered at the sight of him.

"Did you know your boyfriend wears the same three outfits over and over?" She demanded; her eyes already lit with fierce determination.

"Um... yes?"

Poor Parker. I knew that look. She's done this to me countless times. I've always huffed and puffed about it, but I was grateful for her dedication, nonetheless.

"Unacceptable, she said, shaking her head as she rolled up her sleeves, her curled pink hair bouncing against her cheeks. "Parker. Eryn's gonna bring you to my house after school, okay?"

"I um... I don't know if I can," he said quietly, beginning to pick at his nails.

I grabbed his hand, smiling when he looked up in surprise, his eyes wide.

"Don't care. I will not let you wear three outfits! You must have choices!" She said loudly, beginning to walk away, mumbling to herself.

I watched as she drew shapes in the air, not doubting for a second that she was already planning her next piece.

"Eryn?"

"Yes, my dear?"

"Why am I going to her house?"

I looked at him with exaggerated pity plastered on my face. "Oh Parker. She's gonna make you some clothes."

"What?" He took a step back, trying to shake my hand away, but I followed, tightening my grip slightly as I led the way to his first class.

"Sadly, that means you will have to be measured," I told him, fighting a smile. "I know I'll be downright disappointed to see that."

"No," he started, sounding panicky. "I can't do that, I don't know if my parents would let me, and—"

"Parks, look at me," I said, dropping all the teasing I had been pushing. His deep blue eyes finally met mine, and for a split second, I was once again amazed by the emotions he was able to display through his eyes alone. "If you are uncomfortable, tell her, but this is her way of showing love. She wants you to look good, and it makes her happy to know that it was her who provided it for you."

"Yeah… but I just… I don't want to wear a ton of color, and if she um…" he trailed off, shrugging his shoulders. He didn't have to say anything else; I already knew exactly what he was thinking: what if she laughs?

I wiggled my eyebrows at him, trying to make him laugh. "Well, even if she does stuff you into a rainbow-colored onesie, at least we can match!"

He did laugh at that. "You have a rainbow onesie?"

"Of course. And I can assure you," I stage whispered, leaning closer to his ear. "It really makes my butt look amazing."

The bell rang above us, and people's voices rose and fell as they said goodbye to friends and hurried to their classes.

His cheeks were bright red, and a slight smile made its way onto his face, but there was still a look of anxiousness in his eyes.

"Parks. You would look good in anything. Cherry has good taste, don't worry." I suppressed a grin as Parker choked on seemingly nothing, coughing as he looked away, his cheeks lighting up.

"Fine," he said, his voice slightly raspy. "I'll wait for you after school."

"I would hope so, otherwise I'd be devastated, waiting alone in the rain."

"It's not raining."

"Shut up! In the rain!"

His smile was small as he hurried to his class, and soon, I lost sight of his blond head in the crowd.

We drove up to Cherry's driveway in silence. Parker glanced around, his eyebrows furrowed as he saw the wooden figurines hidden in bushes and waiting beside the front door.

"Marissa, Cherry's mom, is a carver," I told him, leaning in. He smelled like pine trees and soap, and I had to stop myself from grabbing him and pulling him closer. "And that means everything smells like wood, and it's amazing."

He didn't say anything. His thumbs were in tatters as he picked at the skin with his nails.

"Hey." I covered his hands with mine, refusing to move as he turned to look at me, jolting in surprise at how close my face was to his. "It'll be okay. I'll be here every step, okay?"

He nodded, squeezing my hand softly, his eyes darting to my lips and back. We stayed like that for a quiet moment, the car creaking as it settled. He looked down, opening the car door and slipping out, letting a rush of cold air hit me.

I ran my hands through my hair and sighed before getting out behind him.

As we stepped closer, we rejoined our hands, sending a flood of warmth to my chest.

I was surprised that he wanted to be this close, especially around strangers.

His eyes were wide as I knocked on the door.

There was a muffled shriek of delight, and a pair of footsteps pounded up to the door. There was a pause, the sound of someone taking a deep breath. After a moment, it flew open, and Marissa leaped out, her eyes wildly excited.

Ah. Cherry told her I have a boyfriend. This'll be fun.

"Eryn! Come in, come in!" She said happily, gesturing for us to come inside.

"Hey Marissa," I started, gently tugging a reluctant Parker into the cozy foyer. "On a scale of one to ten, how excited is Cherry?"

"Oh honey, she's got a little stool for him to stand on and everything," she said, an affectionate smile on her face. "I'd say an eleven."

"Crap."

"And you sweetheart, what's your name?"

I looked back at Parker, realizing that he was awkwardly standing at the door. I kicked off my shoes, and so did he, looking incredibly relieved as he did.

"I'm Parker," he said quietly, his knuckles turning white as he squeezed my hand tighter.

Marissa didn't miss that, she smiled warmly, clapping her hands together softly.

Parker still flinched at the noise.

"Well Parker, it's an absolute pleasure to meet you. Are you hungry?"

I groaned, pulling Parker towards the stairs. "Nope, we're good," I answered, knowing she would stuff us until we passed out in a food coma if we let her.

I felt Parker pause, still holding my hand tight.

"Are you hungry, Parks?"

He stared straight ahead, not looking at anything in particular, and nodded slowly.

Marissa was still for a split second before hurrying to the kitchen, clanging pots and spoons as she made him a bowl of whatever was left over.

"You okay?" I asked quietly, placing my arm across his shoulders.

He looked up at me then, and I saw a flash of fear in his eyes before determination covered every trace.

"Yeah," he whispered. "I'm fine."

He wasn't, I at least knew that, but I nodded, leading him into the kitchen.

Immediately, we were hit with the strong scent of chicken and carrots as we walked through the doorway.

Marissa was pouring a glass of cold lemonade, placing it on the table next to a bowl filled with steamed carrots and barbeque chicken.

Parker let go of my hand, rubbing his own against his jeans nervously, and sat down at the glass table, folding his hands in his lap.

"What's wrong honey?" Marissa asked. "Do you want any bread?"

"No thank you. Thanks for the food," he said softly, and only after Marissa had waved her hand, clearly flattered, did he begin to eat.

I've never seen anyone eat so fast in my entire life. I honestly thought he was going to choke. He would cut the meat and carrots so quickly, and then he would shove them into his mouth. If I'm being totally honest, I think he swallowed them whole, like a freaking lizard.

When he finished the bowl, Marissa was practically glowing with happiness, and she whisked the bowl away, plunking it into the sink with a chuckle.

He took a sip of his lemonade, standing up carefully to move next to me.

"Are you okay?" I asked incredulously.

"Yeah. Just hungry."

"Oh my God, I thought you were going to choke! Did you even chew? When was the last time you ate?"

He shrugged, hiding a small smile as he sipped his drink.

"Mom! Are they here?" I smirked as Cherry's yell echoed down the stairs.

"Yes Cherry! Parker here was just having a snack." She ruffled his hair affectionately. I felt a small burst of amusement as she stretched her arm up to reach the top of his not very tall body.

He froze, eyes wide as he stared into his drink.

"Mom! You were supposed to tell me!"

We heard footsteps slamming down the stairs, and Cherry came careening into the kitchen.

She grabbed Parker's arm and yanked him out and up the stairs before I could say a word.

"I should uh," I jabbed my thumb in the direction they had gone.

"Yes, you really should, he's probably panicking," Marissa said, an affectionate smile on her face.

I nodded, turning to leave.

"Eryn, honey?"

"Yes?" I turned to face her again.

"He's a very sweet boy. I like him. Don't lose him."

I couldn't help but smile, and she patted my cheek, pushing me towards the stairs. I didn't think she would ever know how much that meant to me.

I grew up here. I knew all the best hiding places, I knew that Marissa puts too much soy sauce in everything, I knew that Cherry liked to scream-yawn in the morning, but I always forgot how much they knew about me.

They liked him. How could I ask for more?

I suddenly heard ripping of fabric, and I broke into a run.

I burst into Cherry's room. Cherry screamed, dropping the pin she had been holding.

"Eryn! You egg, help me pick them up!" She yelled, bending over and beginning to pick them up, one by one.

I ignored her, moving around the pins and looking up at Parker, who was standing on the stool Marissa had told us about.

It had an old unicorn sticker on the leg.

"Hey Parks, you're finally taller than me!" I exclaimed, hugging his torso.

"Shut up," he scoffed, his eyes following Cherry carefully.

"Well I never!" I gasped, looking up at him with a mock offended expression.

A flicker of a smile passed over his face, like a candle in the wind, and I felt tingles in my toes.

"What happened?" I asked, turning to see that Cherry had finished picking up the pins and was now at her desk, holding up a piece of paper with different splatters of colors and scrutinizing now they looked next to Parker's nervous form.

She grunted, pointing to the corner where the light green jacket Parker had been wearing laid in tatters.

"Wha—hey, he was wearing that!" I said loudly, hurrying to pick it up and hold it close.

She had literally torn it in half, and the shirt he was

currently wearing seemed doomed.

I brought the destroyed jacket over to Cherry's bed, sitting down with it.

It smelled like him, and as weird as it sounded, it settled my mind.

"He said it was fine," she said, patting his leg without looking. He flinched and nearly fell backwards off the stool, arms whirling to keep himself up. He straightened, looking mortified. "Besides, it was ugly."

"I liked it," I mumbled, feeling defensive, as if it had been my own. Parker's cheeks lit up in his classic deep red.

"Well I didn't, and it's my opinion that matters here," she said, winking at me as she began measuring the length of Parker's shoulders. "So shut up."

I barked out a laugh, crossing my legs on her mattress and leaned back as Parker stood stone still.

I watched as he rubbed the edge of his thumb up and down the length of his ring finger.

His muscles were tense, and he was biting his lip, squinting like he was trying not to say anything.

"Cherry?" he suddenly asked, picking at his nails now. "When we were um... talking, earlier, you know, at the café, you said you've been depressed?"

"Stop moving," she started, slapping his hands gently. "Yeah. I did say that, didn't I?"

She didn't say anything more, instead humming softly as she picked up a length of dark blue cloth and held it next to his face.

She did this a lot. Or at least she used to. It's always been hard for her to share anything emotional, anything that would make her vulnerable to scrutiny, so she would wait until the silence was unbearable, or someone changed the topic. The latter usually happened, and she would be saved from speaking.

But Parker isn't like that, he wouldn't change the subject for her, he would wait until she was ready.

His very being was quiet, and if Cherry told him that she

had been depressed, if she didn't bristle at his words, she would answer.

Parker stared straight ahead, his face bright red. He closed his eyes for a moment, lips moving like he was talking to someone.

I stayed silent, watching both of them avidly avoid each other's eyes. This was their time. I wouldn't interfere.

Finally, Cherry sighed, turning to face her desk, fumbling with her sewing machine. It was bright pink, almost matching her hair perfectly. Almost.

"Yeah. I've had depression since 6th grade," she said, plastering a fake smile on before turning back to Parker. "I got bullied. Depression was the result. Eventually, I stopped taking it and I fought back."

She wrapped a huge chunk of fabric around his torso, the dark blue immediately making his hair look lighter. She ducked behind him, pinning the ends together.

"It's not that big of a deal, I take meds and go to therapy, but it's a part of me, so I couldn't just ignore it, could I?" Her words were calm, carefully formed and gentle.

Parker's eyes flicked to the floor. "Does... does it still hurt?"

Cherry tilted her head as she spoke around the pins in her mouth. "Yeah. Depression doesn't really go away, but it's not who I am, you know? Like, it's not always painful."

Parker slowly nodded, biting his lip.

Cherry glanced at me, and I smiled, crossing my legs again as I nodded encouragingly.

"Ow!" Parker jolted a bit, and Cherry chuckled.

"Sorry. I usually do this on mannequins." She pointed to her closet, and I followed her finger.

The look of this mannequin made me question life. It had a wig on it! A freaking wig! I didn't scream, but I did jump out of my skin.

"Oh my God!" I yelled, pressing my hand over my heart as Parker and Cherry laughed loudly at my pain.

Over the next hour, Cherry ducked under Parker's arms, twirling blue thread behind her as she made Parker a new shirt from nothing.

Her face was set in deep concentration, but she made small chat with him, talking about teachers and times when she had hunted down and screamed at my exes.

I was the buffer between them, adding commentary and laughing at whatever Cherry had been yelling about.

Parker and Cherry were polar opposites, but they were able to find things to talk about anyway.

Cherry seemed determined to create a conversation with her, and after an eternity of terrible jokes, Parker smiled more, gave longer answers.

The thing about Cherry's sewing skills is that she moves extremely fast. So fast that it only took her two hours to make a shirt store quality.

It's almost impossible for me to do anything that big in that short amount of time. I can barely talk and walk, let alone sew and talk.

"Hey Parker," Cherry started, slyly grinning at me. "Take off your shirt."

"Wha—no!" he said, turning the brightest shade of pink I had ever seen on him.

"It's getting in the way!"

He frowned, glancing at me, but he did as he was requested.

While she worked, I took the time to watch him.

Parker was still, jostling every so often by Cherry's movements.

His forearms were tightly wrapped in white bandages. The cat must've really done a number on him.

When Cherry removed the fabric from around his chest, he glanced at me again, and, catching me watching, quickly asked for a sweatshirt. Cherry rustled around her closet for a while he anxiously waited.

There was a silver scar stretched over his shoulder, as long as the beginning of my palm to the end of my middle finger.

I frowned, wondering where he had gotten it.

I was surprised at the disappointment blooming in my chest as she handed him a bright yellow sweatshirt that had been buried deep in her closet.

I said nothing, his discomfort at me observing him making me stare down at my palms, lost in thought.

Was I doing something wrong?

"Done!" Cherry yelled, slumping in her chair as she chucked the newly made shirt at Parker, who actually fell backwards from where he had been sitting on the stool. "Put it on immediately! Show Eryn how much of a master I am!"

He blushed, turning to face the wall as he stripped Cherry's yellow sweatshirt off and slipped the royal blue shirt on.

He turned to face us now, fumbling with the buttons as his hands shook.

"Here," I said, clambering off the bed and straightening, trying to seem cool. My heart was racing. "Let me help."

He blew a small puff of hair through his nose, his eyes trained on the ground.

As I unbuttoned his shirt up, I couldn't help but grin as the pink from his cheeks spread down his neck and shoulders.

"There," I said, stepping away to see the full glory of him.

The dark blue made his hair look like pure gold, and his eyes looked darker as he watched my reaction, and all at once, I felt my breath whoosh out of me as Cherry patted my shoulder.

"Breathe, lover boy," she laughed, and I sucked air back into my lungs, feeling my ears grow warm.

"Well?" He asked, watching me carefully. "Does it look okay?" I could see his biceps tense beneath the short sleeves.

I opened my mouth to speak, but nothing came out.

How could I even begin to describe how good he looked in that color?

"Right, I shouldn't have come," he mumbled, beginning

to unbutton the shirt as his brows creased.

"No!" He looked up, surprised. "No. I like it. It suits you," I told him, clearing my throat.

He nodded despite his bewildered eyes, his hands dropping beside him once more.

"Where's your um... mirror?" he asked, wringing his hands.

She pointed to the corner of the room, right beside her door, a small satisfied smile on her face.

He made his way over, stepping over abandoned strips of fabric and bent pins.

His eyebrows furrowed as he peered at himself. He turned slightly, blushing when he caught my gaze in the mirror.

"You likey?" Cherry asked, leaping over to him.

He nodded, looking surprised as he did.

"Yay! Mission accomplished!" she shrieked, dancing around the room. "Now get out! You guys should talk about how great I am!"

Parker glanced at his tattered sweatshirt once more and nodded, quietly stepping into the hallway.

"Thanks, Cherry," I said, hugging her. "It looks amazing, he's just nervous."

"I know," she said, smiling as she waved at him from the hallway. "I saw how you were looking at him, all doe-eyed."

"Shut up!" I laughed, shoving her onto her bed.

Marissa sent us off with a bag of leftover chicken, which I gave to Parker.

As I drove him home, the silence grew, pursuing me to tell him, to give him the praise he deserved.

"Parks?" He glanced over, tugging at the short sleeves. "You look amazing. You look really, really good."

"Thanks," he whispered, rubbing the bandages gently.

"They still hurt?"

He nodded, staring out the window.

"Damn cats, huh?"

"Yeah," he said after a moment. "Damn cats."

Bella Van Winkle

I dropped him off at the mailbox, and when I pulled away, I watched him through the rearview mirror.

He stayed still, his hair lit up from my fading headlights.

I wanted to turn around, to lift him into the air and kiss him senseless, but I didn't. Why would I? We haven't gotten any farther than a kiss to the top of his head.

How could I scare him away like that? Answer: I couldn't. Wouldn't, more like.

He wanted to wait. And that's okay. I would wait for him, even if the sky fell in the meantime.

I mean, look at him. With eyes like his, anyone would, but I was so glad that it was me who would be waiting.

chapter ten
that went well

Parker

Weeks went by in a blur, and each day felt more normal than the last.

Eryn made me feel strangely happy, and the longer we were together, the less scared to live I was.

Today, we were in the tree. We weren't talking, but we didn't have to. His presence made me calm, it made the world stop spinning.

The sun was setting, the sky splattered with pink and orange like an artist had painted the sky with a brush made for masterpieces. Eryn's hair looked like melted chocolate as the sun shone its last rays of light rightfully onto him.

As the sun disappeared, the cold reappeared, but we were prepared. I was wearing his leather jacket over my sweatshirt, and he was wearing his own sweatshirt. We were leaning against each other, something Eryn had insisted we do to save warmth.

He claimed he was warm. I wasn't sure if I believed him.

"Tell me a story," Eryn said, sighing as he shifted, leaning heavier onto me.

"What kind of story?" I asked, knocking my foot against his.

"A real one."

"You don't want to hear any of my stories, they don't exactly end happily."

"So? That's the best part: they're real. Real life doesn't always end happily."

"I don't think so."

"Please?"

"I really don't want to."

He leaned forward, forcing me to move away. His ears were turning pink, which was never a good sign.

"Why? You listened to my stories, why won't you allow me to listen to yours? I want to be here for you like you were for me."

"Because I said no," I said, pulling my feet away from him.

"Stop doing that," he said, scowling at my legs.

"Doing what?"

"You always pull away! I can't ever talk to you, you just shut down. Do you care? About us? Is that something you just don't want to talk about?"

"You don't know me. Stop assuming you do."

"You won't let me know you!"

"Just stop talking. I don't want to talk about this." I told him, getting up to leave.

"Why are you being like this? We've been together for a while now, and you've never told me anything about you!" He got up too, stepping close to me. "I don't even know your last name."

I shook my head at him, looking up. He was my ride, I couldn't leave without him.

Eryn leaned forward, grabbing my hands. "Talk to me."

"You don't know anything about me," I growled, ripping my hands from his grasp.

"I know a lot more than you think," he said loudly. "You just don't care enough to tell me."

"Why do you need to know? It's my life and my business and you'd be better off not knowing anyway." I crossed my arms, fuming. He mirrored my movements.

I've never seen him like this. His eyebrows were furrowed, and his eyes narrowed. He wouldn't relent until I did.

Not that I cared. He was being rude, and invasive. So what if he told me about his life? That was his choice, I'm not obligated to tell him anything.

In the back of my mind, buried under all the anger, I was tired. I didn't want to do this. Anything but this.

"You're being ridiculous," he said quietly. "How could you have been so bold on the first day I met you? Do you remember?"

I didn't say anything.

"You asked me what to get. I told you something chocolate, perfect for the rain." His voice grew louder. For once, the loudness of it didn't make me flinch. "You said chocolate it is, and you ordered a mocha and a chocolate chip cookie."

"That's not being bold; that's asking for advice, then taking it."

"Then why can't you do the same now?" He was grappling for words I wouldn't give him. I could feel myself getting closer and closer to my breaking point, but I wouldn't let him force me to give up everything I've been trying so hard to hide.

"Eryn, just stop. You know this isn't the same situation, it's not fair of you to bring that up."

"Quit being scared of nothing!"

My eyes snapped open. I'm going to regret this.

"You wanna know so badly? Huh? It's Sheil, okay? My last name is Sheil, but I don't want to be a Sheil, because my dad hates me," I yelled, getting close to Eryn's stone-cold face. "Because I'm gay, alright? He hates me, he will never appreciate my existence even though he made me! Do you know what that feels like Eryn? My mom doesn't care either, and neither does anyone *ever* at school. I don't have a single friend, I don't have anything, and you think you have the right to tell me I'm scared of nothing? You have no idea." My hands were shaking.

He was quiet for a second, breathing hard through his nose and staring at me with fiery eyes.

"I can help you Parks—"

"Don't call me that."

"If you would just—"

"I don't want your help! I don't want it, you'll just get in the way." I turned away from his hurt face and started to climb down the tree. I didn't care if he gave me a ride anymore. There was no way I'd be able to get in a car with him anyway.

"Come on, I'm trying so hard to make us work, but—"

"I don't need you."

The sound of Eryn's small intake of breath was almost too much for me to bear, and I nearly turned around, raced back up the tree and begged him for forgiveness, to love me like no one else would.

But I didn't.

"Then maybe we should stop seeing each other," he said quietly.

I looked up at him from the ground, the ground that stuck to the bottom of my shoes, the ground that was littered with fallen willow leaves and pine needles.

He was clenching his fists, but he looked exhausted. My own heart was dragging me so far down I could've been crawling. I should've been, but I wasn't.

"Maybe we should," I said.

He watched me carefully, his shoulders sagging. He didn't move, and somehow, that hurt more than the fact that we wouldn't be together anymore.

I felt my heart shatter into a million pieces, just like the mug had in the café so long ago, except this time, Eryn wouldn't be here to help me clean it up.

We stared at each other for a moment, hungrily taking

each other in, like we would never see each other again.

Maybe we wouldn't. That's the most screwed up part.

I shrugged off his leather jacket. Eryn said it had powers, but I can't see them working on me.

I don't deserve them.

I dropped it on the ground, hoping he would stop me from leaving. I knew he wouldn't.

Eryn pursed his lips, turning to duck under the veil of leaves, returning to the heart of my haven tree, and I turned to leave.

It was too good to be true anyway.

On my way home, thoughts were whirling around my mind like a hurricane, piercing wherever they hit.

When I arrive home, Father was with Mom. They were on the couch together, laughing at something he had said. They reminded me of him, but I knew we would never do what they have done to me.

A baseball game blared in the background.

When Father saw me, he grunted and moved away from Mom, saying I had ruined the mood. I brushed my hands against my pants, knowing that tonight, I had come home too late, too early, too much or little amount of time that would allow them to pretend I wasn't real.

Mom shot me a look before she caught herself, forcing herself to look sympathetic. I could still see the corners of her mouth turning down, and the way she ever so slightly narrowed her eyes.

I was numb. I didn't feel hurt or angry or glad to be home or anything. I couldn't force myself to feel anything. Worst of all, this was normal. I felt this every day of my life, never skipping even an hour. I wished I could scream, throw myself onto the ground and drag Eryn here from the heaven he belonged in, tell him everything that was wrong with me. But I didn't move at all.

"Where were you all day, huh?" Father suddenly yelled, slamming his hand on the table.

I flinched, smelling whiskey on his breath and realizing how different Eryn's loud voice was to Father's.

"I'm sorry, I-I was—" I started.

"Oh you're sorry, huh? So sorry, sorry that you're late, sorry that you ruined our entire damn lives too, right?" He stepped closer, his shadow cast from the TV covering the light and making him seem like a giant. I wonder if I'll survive this one.

I glanced behind him at Mom, silently begging her for help.

She stood stoic, finally looking determined, but now, it was for the wrong reasons. Mother shook her head.

"I'm sorry," I whispered.

"If you say sorry one more time, I'll make you sorry you were ever born," Father said, his voice terrifying low.

I closed my mouth, swallowing nervously.

If I say nothing, am I doing the right thing? Eryn forced me to talk, forced me to share whatever plagued my mind. I forgot that in most places, I am not allowed to do so. I should've been more cautious.

"What, you're not gonna say anything?" he roared, reaching back and punching me in the face, square on my cheekbone.

I collapsed to the ground, my hands coming up to cover my head. My ears started ringing, my cheek pounding in waves of pain to match my heartbeat that I could suddenly feel on my dry tongue.

He had never laid his hands on me before.

It's my fault. I shouldn't have provoked him, I should've stayed out longer.

I heard my father screaming, telling me to get out of his house so distantly it was like I wasn't here.

My legs carried me out of the house before I even realized I was moving, houses that I have grown up next to becoming a blur as I moved faster and faster than I had ever been. The trees beside me became streaks of dark green that I couldn't focus on through my pounding footsteps.

I fell on the ground, blocks away from where I had once lived, in a little space between trees and was silent.

I can't do this anymore. There isn't a point to any of this crap, this thing people on the streets called life.

My parents hate me. They don't want me around, but they made me! They made me and raised me, taught me to talk, rejoiced in my first words and sent me off to the first day of school with an encouraging farewell, and they just decided they didn't want me? How could they?

I don't have any friends, except for... I don't have any friends.

I'm being bullied at a school that I hate being at, and everyone around me just laughs at me. Not one... barely anyone ever stood up for me.

Now Eryn doesn't want me either.

No one wants me.

I'm tired. The world is too much for me, too cruel, too heartbreaking, too unforgiving for someone like me.

My legs picked me up once more and carried me away.

I give up.

chapter eleven

336

Eryn

I could hear Stepmonster in the other room, and the dishes clinking together in the kitchen. I didn't care too much about the noise or the unpleasant fact that Stepmonster was home. As long as Mom was safe, I could be upset alone.

I stared at his contact picture. I should've told him how beautiful he was before he left.

I closed my eyes, resting my phone on my chest.

Maybe it was wrong to break up with him. I didn't want to, but he was so angry, I didn't know what else to do.

I'd been just as mad as he had been, but something about him made me hold myself back. Something about him has always made me hold everything—everything that I would usually let come roaring to the surface like a dragon—back.

The look in his eyes when he whipped around, finally telling me the things I have always been curious about, was nothing less than extraordinary. If he wanted to, I'm positive he would take over the world. There has always been a blazing fire in his eyes, and it's always made him more real than anything I have ever known.

Now, I don't get to see him anymore.

His dad hated him? Just like mine, although Stepmonster wasn't exactly my dad, and he will never be.

Why would that idiot push me away? I've told him over and over again that I'm here for him, but he doesn't want me. He doesn't want anyone, and that hurt more than the knowledge that he was unwilling to let himself change.

"Damnit," I groaned, digging the heels of my hands into my eyes.

He never shared anything with me anyway. I practically shared my life story with him, and he didn't tell me anything about himself, no matter how many times I asked him.

I guess I just wanted him to trust me, like I had trusted him.

Maybe this was all in my head. Maybe he didn't like me the way I liked him.

He made my head spin as first, his very smile made me feel dizzy. Every time he walked into a room, I swear I had a stroke.

After a while, Parker just made me calm. He helped me think, and instead of getting mad, he made me hold myself back. How could he know how to do that for me?

What would happen now that he was gone?

My phone dinged quietly. I sighed, jolted out of my thoughts a bit too suddenly before picking it up.

It was from Cherry. She'd asked me if I'd heard from Parker.

Eryn: No, we broke up like 2 hours ago :(

Eryn: Why? Do you need him for something?

Cherry: Oh God

Eryn: What's wrong?

Cherry: Check your messages are any from him?

I rolled my eyes before searching through my unread messages.

There was one from him, delivered about an hour ago.

My heart dropped as I opened it, and cold sweat dripped

down my back as I read the words that he had typed out.

Parker: Hey Eryn. You won't look at this until it's too late hopefully. I wanted to tell you that I'm sorry for doing this to you. I'm pretty sure you were the only person who cared about me. I have to do this. I don't have any other way. I know you tried to help, that you wanted to, but there's no way you could have. No one could. My dad hates me and my mom gave up on me too. They finally kicked me out. I really have nothing left now. There's no point. I'm sorry.

Parker: I am so sorry.

No. No. No, he couldn't have, he wouldn't. Would he?

Cherry's name popped up on the screen, and I scrambled to click on it.

Cherry: He's at the hospital, if you found it.

Eryn: Alive??

Cherry: I don't know, I'm headed over there now

The despair that had weighed so heavily on my chest that I couldn't breathe suddenly switched.

Rage. I was livid.

I grabbed my bedside table and threw across the room, ripping the outlet of the wall in the process, reveling in the loud crash.

I put on shoes and my leather jacket that Parker had—

Grabbing my phone, I slammed my door behind me, storming towards the kitchen.

Mom looked up from the sink, shock plastered across her thin face.

"Eryn, what happened? There was a big crash and—"

"I'm leaving."

She stepped back suddenly, dropping the sponge she had held.

"What do you mean?" she asked quietly, wringing her hands as she looked up at me.

"Something happened to Parker," I told her, my whole everything screaming to run to him. "He's in the hospital, I need to see if he's alive."

"Who's Parker?"

For the second time today, my heart slams to a stop. How could I not have told her? Parker, my entire world, I wanted to say, Parker, my everything that actually matters, Parker, the person who cared.

"He's my boyfriend," I said, feeling lightheaded.

She blinked and smiled. I haven't seen her smile like that in a long time.

"Go get him. Don't let him get away."

I hugged her roughly, and she squeezed me tight, just like she had when Stepmonster wasn't here, when everything he had done hadn't happened yet.

"Mom, I don't know what to do," I whispered into her shoulder, squeezing my eyes shut.

She nodded, rubbing my back in soothing circles. "I don't know who this boy is, but in the past month or so, I've never seen you happier. The best thing you can do right now, is to go to him. Don't lose him."

Next thing I knew, I was on my way to the hospital, my fingernails digging into the steering wheel so hard they left marks.

My fingers were twitching almost violently, enough that when I flipped the blinker, it took a couple tries to actually make anything happen.

I couldn't stop thinking about him. The way his hair looked like in the setting sun earlier tonight, the way his hand fit mine, the way his cheeks turned pink when I complimented him, the way his footsteps sounded when I walked next to him. The way his presence had felt.

It's one thing to lose him in a breakup, but it's a completely different thing to lose him to—

Nausea rose suddenly into my throat and forced me to pull over.

I scrambled out of the car, racing over the guardrail, and, leaning over it, threw up whatever little things I had eaten today.

The sun was almost gone, but the darkness didn't obscure

my vision; I was already blind in my rage.

How dare he? He couldn't do this. I hated that he would do this to me, to himself, I didn't want to lose him— I *couldn't* lose him.

The unearthly silence of my car welcomed me back, and I stared straight ahead, forcing all emotion back until all that was left behind was anger.

I may not know how to control myself now, but anger was something that I have taken comfort in for a very long time.

I haven't been to the hospital since I was a little kid and broke my arm falling from a tree, but I don't remember it looking so ominous.

The sky opened and released its own despairing tears as I rushed to the doors, praying I wasn't too late.

The waiting room would have been almost silent if not for the bubbling tank holding peaceful fish in the corner of the room.

It didn't deserve to be peaceful. Not now. Not when the sun was in one of those rooms.

My breathing seemed deafening as I sprinted to the front desk, gasping for air as I reached it.

A bored woman sat behind the counter, typing something into the computer in front of her.

"How can I help you," she droned, tearing bloodshot eyes away from the screen to look up at me.

"Where's— sorry, I need a room number?" I asked, my entire body tense.

"Who's the patient."

"Uh, Parker Sheil?"

"Parker?" She looked up, surprised.

"Yeah," I said, grateful for the interested look on her face.

"Poor kid. Used to be a regular. He's really roughed himself up. Come to think of it, you being here for him has officially made you and the girl who just came in more people waiting for him than he's ever had."

I felt something snap in my chest and I couldn't hold back the torrential waves that threatened to overtake me.

"The number!" I yelled, slamming my hands down onto her countertop. "Give me the number now, I need it, I need it, give to me, please!"

"Sir, I need you to calm down," she said, reaching for the phone.

"I really don't need to calm down, I don't need anything except for that number, I need to see him! Why isn't anyone listening?" I yelled, pulling my hair.

"Security, we have a situation at the front desk," she mumbled into the phone, standing up.

This stranger had no idea, absolutely no idea what he had done, no idea what he would do in the future, and what he meant to me.

"Shut up! Shut up, just give me the room number!"

"I'm sorry sir, family only," she said sternly.

A couple of security guards walked in behind me, their boots making their footsteps sound more important and I couldn't focus on anything else but the fact that *his* were the footsteps I needed to hear. They stepped behind me, pulling my arms roughly and beginning to drag me out.

A kid in the waiting room started to cry, his blubbering sobs almost too loud for me to bear. His mother shushed him, holding him close to her chest. Did his mom ever do that for him?

"I *am* his family!" I screamed, going limp with utter despair.

"Hold on. Explain," the woman said quietly, holding up a hand. The security guards paused.

"I just need to see him. He's my boyfriend, I just need to know he's okay." I looked up at her. She was pressing her lips into a firm line. "Please. I need him."

She curtly nodded, waving her hand in the air.

"Room 336."

I nodded weakly, thanking her before wrenching my arms

away from the guards and hurrying into the elevator.

It was too quiet. The elevator didn't have any music to block my thoughts. Maybe they knew people like me couldn't deal with music in this place.

With my body finally still, I was forced to think.

I wonder if he actually cared about me. Maybe he just wanted me to feel his loss.

In this place, the hospital, I was overwhelmingly aware of how many lives were lost here, whether in a fight to the death for their very being against a fatal disease or from something they did to themselves.

This was no place that I wanted to be. This was no place he should be.

I let out a shaky breath. I remember how grief had made Mom act when my dad left. She wouldn't leave the house for days, and when she did, something always happened to make her return home once more.

I don't want to feel the same loss as she did.

The closer the elevator got to his floor, the more terrified I became. I wished I was afraid of how the elevator shook slightly as it rose, thinking about the cables twitching as they struggled to release themselves from the horrid grasp of a metal death box, but I couldn't possibly imagine the fear someone else would have felt. Nothing was scarier than what I was about to face.

I prayed and begged anyone who could have been listening for Parker to have failed, for him to still be here, for him to be alive.

I need to be with him, feel his joy sink into my cold skin like he had once been able to do.

The elevator shook as it stopped. I gripped my jacket tighter, needing its strength now more than ever.

I felt as if the floor would swallow me whole if I stepped off. Perhaps it would, and I would be forced to stay here, not knowing whether or not if he was alright.

I don't want to lose him. I *can't* lose him.

The doors slid open, and a blur of pink tackled me to the

wall.

"Eryn! Eryn oh god, oh god," Cherry sobbed, holding me tight.

I squeezed her just as hard, surprised at the relief that flowed through me the moment I realized it had been her.

"Go see him," she said, pulling away and wiping her eyes.

"Is he…?" I trailed off, my chest tight.

She refused to look at me, tucking her hair behind her ears

"Go see him," she whispered, walking into the waiting room.

My breath caught in my throat, and all of a sudden, I couldn't breathe. I stumbled out of the metal death box I had prayed in, staring at her wildly. She pointed to the door behind her. The numbers 336 were silver, like they knew he needed a room fit for a prince. There wasn't anyone else in the waiting room. Just us and the presence he left behind.

"How did you know?" I asked, rushing to her and gripping her arms.

"He was on the news," she started, tears welling in her small brown eyes. "They said he was fatally injured and homeless and that if his parents recognized him, they needed to bring him home."

"The news? Why would they…?"

"I don't know. We'll figure it out later."

Staggering towards his room, I started to turn the doorknob, but stopped. My chest felt heavy, like someone was standing on me. This was too much for me, I couldn't do this, how could I? How would I survive the idea of him?

"Go, Eryn. It'll be okay," Cherry said softly.

Holding my breath, I pushed open the door and stepped in, turning quickly to face the light brown wood as I closed it.

The beeping of the heart monitor was so loud in this silent room; I felt like it was vibrating my brain.

But the monitor means he's alive. I can't tell if that makes me relieved or even more terrified than I already was.

I almost couldn't move. All the rage I had been forcing

myself to feel fell away, and I was suddenly afraid this is how I would remember him.

I forced myself to turn, almost expecting to see an empty bed.

He was pale. He was so pale, and his eyes were closed. He seemed so dull. This was no longer the mighty mouse I knew.

He looked so small in his bed, blankets hanging off the sides and the pillows fluffed like he wasn't there at all.

There was a large bruise and a small cut on his cheek that hadn't been there when we fought only a couple hours ago.

Tears burned my eyes, and I clenched and unclenched my fists, trying to regain the control that I knew I didn't have.

His chest moved up and down slowly, like he was asleep, but this was much worse than sleep. This time, he may not wake up.

I let out a sob, falling to my knees in this cold room, pressing my forehead against the tiles.

"Oh God, Parker," I whispered. "Oh, Parker."

I crawled to his bedside, grabbing his dry and limp hand.

His arms were covered in thick white bandages, but I could see red seeping into them. I didn't want to think about how he had gotten them to bleed like that.

"Please, Parks," I sobbed, pressing his hand to my cheek. "Please don't leave me."

My tears followed an invisible line down his arm, leaving proof of my existence on his skin.

"I need you. God, Parks, I need you."

Opening my eyes, I swept his golden hair from his forehead with a shaking hand.

"You... I'm so mad at you," I whispered, his face blurry. "You should've told me before, you should've trusted me. You should've *told* me."

I leaned closer to his face, my thumb caressing his cheek. His freckles looked so much darker in this lighting.

I should've told him how much I loved him. If I ever got the chance again—

"I love you. I love you so much," I told him, pressing his

hand to my forehead and squeezing my eyes shut.

My whispered confession hung above us like a falling star, but he wouldn't get to see it land. Would he ever be able to hear everything I wanted to tell him? I wanted to tell him how the world turns, the amount of pressure the ocean holds, the way I had gotten my car for much cheaper than I should have. Will he ever hear my words again?

"Don't forget me. Please, please don't forget me, Parks. I love you."

I stroked his hair, shaking from the force of my sobs.

I might never see him again. I don't want to remember him like this, wires and tubes hooking him up to machines, alone in a small, cold room.

I'll never see his baby pictures from when he wasn't plagued with the sickness of life, and I'll never see him read another book or tell an awful joke that makes me groan, and I will never get to bask in the life he gives off again.

I was filled with such a strong need to tell him everything I had ever thought about him. I wanted to tell him how easy it was to smile with him around, how colorful everything seemed around him, how his laugh echoed in my usually busy mind and how his smile was brighter and more real than anything I have ever experienced.

I rested my head against his leg, sobbing for him, cursing anything that could ever keep him down like this.

I watched him breathe for so long, terrified that he would stop, terrified that he would miss a second of the oxygen he deserved to breathe.

His eyelids fluttered as I watched, and I jumped, gripping his hand tight.

"Water," he whispered, his eyes still closed.

"Yeah," I mumbled, grabbing a cup and pitcher that had been left on the bedside table.

I brought it to his dry lips, helping him take a sip.

He furrowed his eyebrows slightly, showing the creases I had grown so familiar with and moved his head to the side. I took the cup away and caressed the side of his face again.

"Mom?" He whispered, his voice raspy.

I held back a sob.

"No Parks, it's Eryn," I told him, my throat aching.

He opened his eyes a sliver, his once bright blue eyes that had twinkled when he laughed no dull.

"Sorry," he whispered. I shook my head, choking on tears. "It's okay. It's okay, Parks."

He shook his head a bit. "No, it's not."

His voice was so quiet I could barely hear him.

"No. It's not," I responded, just as quiet.

"Eryn?"

"Yes?"

He swallowed, closing his dull eyes. "I wasn't ever enough. I can't ever be good enough."

"Parker," I started, brushing more of his thick hair out of his eyes. "You're enough for me."

"You only say that because now you've seen how bad it's been." Parker's eyes bounced around his empty hospital room. "Because I'm here."

"Parks." I tried to catch his attention. Finally, his eyes found mine, and I stared into his eyes that had once held everything. "You have always been enough, since the first moment I knew you existed. I've never wanted anything more than who you are now."

I brushed away the tear that fell from his drooping eyes.

He reached out for me and pressed his hand against my cheek, his arm shaking with the effort. I squeezed my eyes shut and covered his hand with mine.

"I love you," he whispered, pulling me closer.

His scent of laundry detergent and pine lingered under the chemicals that covered his now weak body.

I took another deep breath, opening my eyes to see Parker, drugged up and near death, but alive all the same.

"I've loved you since the very beginning."

I wish this moment could've been different. I wish we were in my room, or in his tree. I wish he was safe in my grasp when he finally told me he loved me.

I wished he'd known I would do anything for him before he...

His breath was shaky on my lips, but I reveled in the fact that there was breath here at all.

"I don't want to lose you," I whispered.

"You won't."

"You don't know that."

The doors flew open behind us, and that's when I realized how fast the heart monitor was beeping.

"What's happening?" I asked, trying to look behind me.

Nurses and doctors were talking loudly all around us, moving in a frenzy of noise, but Parker weakly pulled me closer, and I leaned in to hear him better, my own heart racing.

He pressed his lips against mine, and I felt every promise I have ever thought about telling him rush to the surface.

I closed my eyes, savoring the warmth he emitted. I didn't think our first kiss would be like this.

"Honey, you're gonna have to go, you're making his heart rate shoot up, it could seriously damage his health in his current state." A nurse said from behind me.

Furiously happy and terrified, I kissed Parker one more time before being ushered out of the room.

Cherry stood up as I stumbled back into the waiting room.

We stood silently for a moment—her staring at my red and blotchy face and me staring at the fear in hers.

My face screwed up and I burst into tears again, officially crying more today than I had cried in years.

Cherry rushed towards me, pulling me to the chairs that waited for both of us and hugged me tightly. She whispered comforts, rubbing my back and holding my head to her shoulder as I sobbed.

My chest ached, my whole body felt weak and my head hurt, but I couldn't spare the breath to even thank her. I just let her hold me, my eyes dry and heavy.

She never stopped whispering, and eventually, I fell asleep around 2 am, surrounded by the overwhelming feeling of love for Cherry and Parker.

For the next week, Parker stayed in bed, waking up for a couple hours before falling asleep for much longer than I thought possible.

They had to pump his stomach before I was able to get to the hospital. He almost didn't make it, partly because of the pump but mostly from the deep infected wound on his forearms. I didn't know how they had gotten there, but he hadn't told me yet, so I wasn't going to ask. After everything that had happened, I was going to let him take his time to tell me.

I never left the hospital. I mean, Cherry did drag me to her house to shower once or twice, but I came back as quick as I could afterwards.

After the longest week of my life, he was standing up and walking again. He'd come out into the waiting room where I was napping and kissed me.

He seemed more determined than he had ever been for all the time I've known him.

After a week and a half, they let him go home. He didn't.

He signed himself into a mental health support group that was able to keep him from hurting himself. I'd already had a suspicion that he had been hurting himself, but it was painful to hear it was still happening.

He had called me into his room before they allowed him to leave. His sweatshirt had been laying on the bed, and I remember how excited I was for him to leave this hellhole.

"Eryn," he'd started. "I want to be honest with you."

"Okay, great," I'd responded.

"I uh… this is harder than I thought." His hands had been shaking so hard that I was worried he'd shatter. "I've been cutting myself. For years."

He'd looked at me with his impossibly blue eyes so carefully, like after all this he expected me to leave now.

I had grabbed him and crushed his body against mine. I

told him I didn't care, that he was not alone in this, I would be here to help.

He didn't cry, he just hugged me tighter.

Even when I think of it now, I see the boiling clouds above me as I ran inside, what that kid looked like when I started yelling, how empty that waiting room was. How shiny the number 336 had been on his door.

When something like this happens, you remember every detail.

I'm not happy he did this to himself. He couldn't have done anything worse, and as much as I love him, it really messed me up.

For months, when someone called or texted me unexpectedly, I jumped to my feet, my heart racing, even if Parker was right next to me. If I didn't hear from him for a day, I was a nervous wreck, panicking, expecting the worse and I would search for him, praying I wouldn't find him on the ground somewhere, abandoned and half alive.

Sometimes, he held me instead of me holding him.

When he left for the mental health support group, I was more alone than I had ever been. Stepmonster was drunker and angrier than ever, leaving bottles in his destructive wake. Mom showed up to breakfast with bruises under her ears and a small voice that tells me it's time for school on weekends.

Today was the last, I told myself as I woke up.

I packed my bag with everything I could fit, clothes and small things I couldn't leave behind and left it in my room. I slunk into Mom's room and did the same, placing it beside my own bag in my room.

The kitchen should've been silent, the sounds of coffee brewing and the low classical music filling the atmosphere as Mom did the dishes, but Stepmonster had made sure that that was not an option. He was yelling and laughing with food spilling out of his mouth as he watched TV in the living room.

I quickly walked into the kitchen, who was cooking at the stove, grabbing her arm gently.

"Let's go," I whispered.

Her eyes widened as she glanced behind me and shook her head.

"Mom, I've already packed our bags. I can't do this anymore. I don't like your bruises, and you shouldn't have any bruises anyway! I know how long we've been here, and believe me, if we didn't have to, I wouldn't leave this place, but things have changed. He's made sure of that," I told her, pointing into the living room. Her gaze followed my index finger. "Anywhere would be better than here."

Mom's gaze snapped to mine, and I could already see the reason why we needed to stay on the tip of her tongue, but she said nothing.

She was someone I couldn't leave without. If she wasn't willing to leave, I would be forced to stay too. She knows that. Despite Mom's poor judgment, she was a good mother who loved her son, and her son came first. I came first.

I watched as every plea I have ever made to leave suddenly sunk in, and the switch finally slipped.

She set her spatula down and nodded, wringing her hands nervously.

"Anything for my baby," she whispered.

She began tying up her black hair, her breath shaking a bit and her hands fumbled with the hairband, but she was determined, something I know she had craved for a very long time.

I nodded as I hurrying to my room to grab our suitcases.

I slipped out the front door and ran to my car, throwing the cases into the back. I checked the glovebox, making sure everything we needed was here before starting the car and headed back inside.

I heard the yelling before I opened the door.

I've heard this too many times. Her whimpers and pleads were too much, adding to the pile of blackened memories that was already overflowing.

Day after day, my mother suffered so I wouldn't have to, not once letting me take the blows so she could rest. Her bruises were always black and blue, and if I couldn't see them on her body, they were always hidden away. They were almost permanent.

My legs were already racing towards her, the sound of his voice filling my brain, blowing up like a balloon that had been filled with too much air, and now was the time when it popped. I wouldn't let him do this anymore.

His fat fingers were pressing into the bruises under her ears, strangling the breath from her while holding her, red and gasping, close to his face and yelling demands, screaming insults into her tear-stained face.

I tackled him before I stopped to think about the consequences, feeling my arms wrap around his neck and pulling him back.

Mom sucked in a huge breath as his fingers slipped away from her throat, and Stepmonster struggled to gain control, gargling his words like mouthwash, but he was too hungover and too out of shape to move quickly. It was Saturday, after all.

He tried to wrap his hands around my neck, but I watched as Mom threw a plate at his head before his arms got even close to me.

He cried out in pain as it shattered on his thick skull, dropping around him like rain.

I struggled to my feet, grabbing my shaken mother's hand and running as fast as I could, pulling her along with me.

I practically threw her into the car as I heard Stepmonster roar and stomp outside.

"Mom, I need you to trust me," I yelled, getting in the driver's seat.

"Why? Honey, where are we gonna go?" Mom yelled back, screaming as Stepmonster slammed his fists on the hood of the car, denting the metal.

The car's wheels squealed as I peeled out of the driveway of my childhood home and we watched as it disappeared behind a cloud of dirt.

After a moment of silence, I looked over at her. She was

staring behind us, her breath rushing out of her in breaths that nearly seemed fake.

"I just need you to trust me," I told her.

She watched me for a moment before nodding, shaking her head as she readied herself for our next move.

Mom didn't shed one tear as she climbed into the backseat to change into jeans she hadn't worn in years.

How could so much happen in so little time?

Is this real? Finally, my mom is free from his terrible grasp on her life. She can live as she wants, and so can I.

While I drove, I imagined new beginnings. Christmas with Marissa, Cherry and Mom while Parker tears open my presents for me, making jokes until he cries laughing, watching from the other room as Mom and Parker talk while making the rolls she used to make every Thanksgiving.

I can't wait for the life I will spend with them.

Marissa and Cherry were standing outside their house when we pulled up, arms crossed.

I heard Mom's breath quicken.

"You gonna be okay?" I asked, turning to her.

She stared straight ahead, locking eye contact with Marissa and nodded. "I will have to be. It's time to apologize, baby."

She got out slowly, taking great care as she winced when her bare feet touched the cold ground.

I made my way to Cherry, giving her a hug and a wary look as we watched the exchange unfolding before us.

"It'll be fine," Cherry said, nudging me in the ribs.

"I know. I'm just nervous, it's been a really long time since they saw each other," I told her, folding my arms as well.

Mom stood in front of Marissa, her bruises more evident in the daylight. They watched each other carefully.

"Mare, I know I should have kept in contact with you—" She stopped as Marissa held up her hand.

"Yes Elizabeth, you really should have. I love your son like my own, but he comes over so often that he has a toothbrush and some of his clothes in Cherry's bathroom. You should've come as well! Family sticks together, and you must have remembered the promise we made to each other as teenagers." Cherry and I exchanged a nervous look.

"Of course I do! I wanted to keep him close, I wanted him to have a good life, but I couldn't while he was there!" Mom said back, stepping closer and she gestured wildly. "You have always been the safest place for him to go. I've always trusted you. You know better than anyone that I have always wanted for us to be a family. I still want that."

"So do I," Marissa said, a nostalgic look in her eyes.

"I'm sorry," Mom said, a tear dripping off her nose.

Marissa clicked her tongue and opened her arms wide. Mom stepped into them slowly, throwing her arms around her friend, two friends finally family.

"Oh honey, you don't have to apologize to me. I just wish you would've let me help."

Realization panged in my chest; Marissa's words painfully familiar.

I glanced at Cherry, who smiled.

"I will now," I heard my mom whisper.

For the first time in a long time, I smiled too.

chapter twelve
sick tattoos
(ten years later)

I groaned as I stretched, blinking sleep from my eyes as the morning sun filled my room from the open window.

"Morning, Princy," Eryn said groggily, his head popping up from beside me.

"Morning," I responded, grinning at his bed head before he kissed my cheek and swung his long legs out of bed.

I watched his muscular back as he stretched like I had, making his way to our kitchen.

I got out of bed too, walking over to the window and watching the bright green leaves on the trees that surrounded our house sway gently in the breeze.

The bright orange poppy that sat on the windowsill was almost blinding as its leaves began to soak up the early morning sun.

It's been ten years since I tried to kill myself.

Let me explain myself. I was so tired. Tired of everything,

of living, of waking up in the morning to walk through the same halls every day just so I could grow up and walk through different hallways every day for a paycheck. I was scared of the future without a home, parents or anyone who could've ever wanted me.

I swallowed a bunch of pills and waited until I passed out, hoping I would die peacefully.

They didn't work in time.

I woke up in the hospital, unsure of how I had gotten there and in so much pain that I wasn't able to see.

They told me my body wouldn't let me vomit the pills back up, so they were forced to pump my stomach. The cuts on my arms were so deep that I'd almost bled out before someone found me, and they had gotten infected as well, a wonderful condition that almost resulted in my death.

They saved me. But I knew I would try again.

They kept giving me a drug that made me sleep, probably to keep me from trying to leave or hurt myself again. I didn't care too much, I liked how it took the pain away, how the sleep stopped my thoughts.

They said if I survived the night I would live. Again, I didn't care. I was just going to try again anyway, so in my mind, everything they were doing to save my life was a waste of supplies they could've used on someone much more important.

I woke up all too soon, but this time I wasn't alone. Eryn was there, crying over me, watching me to make sure I stayed alive. In that moment, I made up my mind. I would stop everything. Cutting, doubting him, doubting me, everything, so I could live with him.

And I did.

I can't tell you how hard it was. The days went by in a blur in the mental health group I had signed myself into. My every move was watched, carefully recorded, everything I picked up was made a note of, everything I ate, how long I took in the bathroom.

I wanted to cut so badly that sometimes it was all I could think about. It was something I used to make myself believe I could control that part of myself that I shouldn't have to control.

Eryn's calls made it easier to find strength to get through the day, and eventually, I did it. I was able to convince them and myself that it was no longer such a drastic problem in my life. When they approved me, I went home. Well, not my home.

I did try to go home. Eryn drove me, and when we arrived, my parents had thrown all of my stuff out the window, and it lay on the grass, broken, smashed, and wet from the morning dew.

The only thing that survived was the orange poppy sprout. The pot had broken around it, but the plant was fine, and I was thankfully able to salvage it.

Cherry had come and helped Eryn and I pick everything up, and I remember looking up to see my mother watching us through the sheer curtains of her bedroom, her lips pressed into a thin line. Eryn looked up too, and he had formed a ball out of mud, then chucked it at her window. It hit her chest with a loud thud, and she had screeched, running to get Father. We were gone before she did, leaving the broken glass from my snow globes on the bright green grass.

I lived with Cherry and her mom, and Eryn and his mom until we all graduated.

Eryn's mom was much happier than the stories he told, she acted just like the way he said she had been when he was a kid. There was always Beethoven floating through the air.

It was crowded and I didn't get much privacy, but I loved it despite. I loved how Marissa and Elizabeth knew what I was thinking from a single glance, I loved that they loved me. They really did, and they made it a point to tell me every day how important I was to them.

I slowly learned to despise the silence that I had once sought out.

Eryn went to the same college as me while Cherry went across the country to learn about and create fashion, something she absolutely adored.

After college, Eryn and I were still together. Of course it was hard, and we argued all the time for awhile, but we talked it out, something neither of us were used to.

To this day, I struggle to remember that I am not my parents, that I wasn't the problem. They were.

I asked Eryn to marry me a week after our college graduation. He said yes while people all around us cheered, but for once, I hadn't cared about the crowd.

Everything is different now in the best way possible. I'm happy now.

Depression never really goes away. Cherry knew it from the very beginning. Of course she did, she knows everything about everyone without asking, it's like she stalks them. True, depression will never leave, but I have help now.

The scars will never go away either. Every once in awhile I still get the urge to cut, but my therapist taught me to squeeze an ice cube in my hand until the urge fades.

I did get tattoos to cover the scars though. It's basically a garden all over my forearms and every inch of my upper arm, and I made sure to get as many colors as possible. I needed to see every color on my body. I don't really look like someone who would get tattoos, but they were a way to allow me to not have to be afraid of them.

I used to have a couple favorite places.

Now, when people ask me about my arms, they mean tattoos and not the scars.

My favorite tattoo is two huge orange poppies on the inside of my forearms. It makes me feel like Eryn is with me wherever I go, and that is one of the greatest gifts I could ever ask for.

My stomach is much weaker now, but I have ways around it. I mean, red sauce is not something I'm able to eat anymore, or anything acidic at all really, but Eryn is very supportive.

He still jumps when someone calls, and on bad days, I am there to help him calm down.

But I'm alive. I wake up every day with Eryn beside me and it's all I've ever wanted.

I grinned when I felt Eryn's arms slide over my shoulders, hugging me to his chest.

"Whatcha thinking about?" he asked as he gently turned me around and slowly led me to the kitchen.

"How much I love you," I told him, laughing at his mock disgusted face.

"Ew gross, you have cooties," he said, leaning away from me, waving his hands in front of him like he was shooing a bee away.

"Not today! I showered last night!" I exclaimed, sniffing myself.

"Then you're probably fine," he said, handing me a cup of coffee and settling down at our dining table.

"No but really. I'm glad we're still together," I said quietly, sitting across from him, taking his hand in mine and squeezing.

"I'm glad you're here," he responded, leaning over the table to kiss me softly.

Now, in this new life of ours, everything was okay. Outside, the summer air was beginning to warm, and I smiled at Eryn as he sat back down, squeezing my hand tight as he took a sip of his coffee. The way he smiled was something I can never explain.

When we got married, we sat in the car, on our way to the airport so we could fly to our honeymoon destination, and I remember how close he held me, whispering how he would build the world for me, telling me how good I looked and how excited he was to be with me for the rest of time. Even now, the thought of his words sends warmth spreading across my body, and I felt my love for him grow and ache as my heart struggled to contain it all.

Don't Forget Me

"I love you," I told him, my eyes dancing over his sleepy eyes and floppy hair as the tender smile I knew and loved appeared.

"I love you too. You know that."

"I do."

We sat at the table together, coffee in our cups, in silence.

We didn't feel the need to talk.

We didn't have to.

suicide resources

United States

National Suicide Prevention Hotline:
1-800-273-8255

National Suicide Prevention Hotline (español):
1-800-273-8255

Crisis Text Line: Text TALK to 741-741

International

Argentina: +5402234930430

Australia: 131114

Austria: 142; for children and young people, 147

Belgium: 106

Bosnia & Herzegovina: 080 05 03 05

Botswana: 3911270

Brazil: 188 for the CVV National Association

Canada: 1.833.456.4566, 5147234000 (Montreal);
18662773553 (outside Montreal)

Croatia: 014833888

Denmark: +4570201201

Egypt: 7621602

Estonia: 3726558088; in Russian 3726555688

Finland: 010 195 202

France: 0145394000

(continued)

Germany: 08001810771

Holland: 09000767

Hong Kong: +852 2382 0000

Hungary: 116123

India: 8888817666

Ireland: +4408457909090

Italy: 800860022

Japan: +810352869090

Mexico: 5255102550

New Zealand: 0800543354

Norway: +4781533300

Philippines: 028969191

Poland: 5270000

Portugal: 21 854 07 40/8 . 96 898 21 50

Russia: 0078202577577

Spain: 914590050

South Africa: 0514445691

Sweden: 46317112400

Switzerland: 143

United Kingdom: 08457909090